THE RENOVATION

A REVERSE HAREM ROMANCE

MIKA LANE

HEADLANDS PUBLISHING

BE THE FIRST TO KNOW...

Want more heat, heart,
and bad boys who know what they're doing?
Join my list and I'll send the steam straight to your inbox,
starting with a deliciously naughty story:

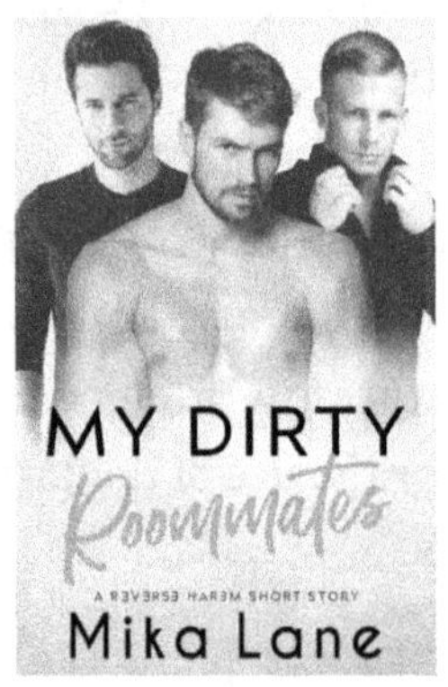

JAYMA

DEAR HOMEOWNER:

A review of our records indicates that your home mortgage loan is in default. Unless payments can be brought current in thirty (30) days, we will take steps to terminate your ownership in the property with foreclosure procedures or other actions to seize the home under the terms of your mortgage agreement.

I didn't bother reading the rest of the notice. I couldn't and besides, I didn't need to. It'd be nothing more than legal mumbo-jumbo and, as it was, I was struggling to catch my breath. I sank down into my sofa and let the letter flutter to the floor, where my cat came over and promptly pissed on it.

I knew I liked that cat.

"Shelle?" I wailed.

"Oh my god. What's wrong? You sound horrible. Are you crying? What the hell happened?"

I blew my nose without pulling the phone away. She was my best friend, and I could blow my nose in her ear if I had to. That's how close we were.

"I got the letter from the bank," I sobbed.

"Letter?" Shelle asked. "What letter? Did you over-draw your account?"

"No! About defaulting on the mortgage." Just saying those words brought the taste of bile to my mouth. I needed water.

"Oooh. Shit, I thought maybe you'd had that straightened out," she said.

"I was hoping, too. You know how Lance and I put the house in my name because I had better credit? Well, now the whole note is mine. That's how it works." I lay back on the sofa. Maybe that would help with my growing nausea.

"Holy shit. He can just bail on the house payments like that? God, I didn't know. But I guess if his name's not on it, he can—"

"Yes, he can, and he did. I can't make the payments myself on my receptionist's salary, and now I'm gonna lose the house. The money I put into it will be gone, my credit will be ruined, and I'll have no place to live. We were supposed to fix it all up and sell it for a nice profit." God, all this crying was giving me a splitting headache.

I hated Lance, that fucker. Gave him three years of my life, and he hooked up with one of his fellow attorneys at the firm. God, I hoped they'd have ugly children some day.

HE'D COME HOME from work, and right away, I sensed something was off. I figured it had been a rough day at work, or maybe he'd been yelled at by the senior partner he worked for. It happened all the time.

My job, on the other hand, as phone-answerer-in-chief at an ad agency, was a breeze. I was done for the day at five p.m. Back at home, dinner usually fell to me. That was fine, though, because I needed to learn to cook anyway. Lance, on the other hand, who was trying to advance at the firm, worked crazy hours. Sometimes late into the night. On occasion, he even slept at the office.

More like he *fucked* at the office, as it turned out.

On that memorable day, when he'd seemed so weird, he started the conversation with, "Jayma, I have something to tell you."

I thought he was joking. You know, pulling my leg. "Pretending" something big was up.

"Can we sit over here?" He pointed to the sofa. Why was he being so stiff?

I added silverware to finish the table setting. "No, babe, dinner's ready. Let's talk here at the table."

"No. No." He raked his hand through his hair. "Let's just sit down over here." Okay, something was really up. He'd not taken off his jacket or tie. Actually, he looked kind of sexy, all suited up. I reached for his hand, thinking I might start a little playing around, but he was already halfway to the sofa. Maybe later, then.

Annoyed he wasn't more enthusiastic about my cooking efforts, I traipsed after him into the living room, which really wasn't much of a room and really wasn't livable, either. There was a hole in the floor that opened to the crawl space under the house, over which we'd placed plastic to block the draft. And so that neither of us stepped there and accidentally fell through, we'd put one of those construction sawhorses up, which we'd stolen from down the street. We planned to put it back when we had a better solution.

I settled into the sofa next to him and, oh, my god! It had finally occurred to me.

He was going to propose!

He squirmed to get comfortable on our lumpy old sofa (why buy a good one when the room wasn't ready yet?) and turned to face me. He seemed not to know what to do with his hands, but finally reached out and held mine. By the fingertips. That was a half-assed handhold if you asked me, but I understood. The pressure! It must have been immense.

The guy was about to propose. He was a mess. It was to be expected.

"Jayma?" He was getting choked up, and his voice broke.

God, I loved him so much at that moment. On the verge of tears as he was proposing. I'd tell our children and grandchildren about this someday.

Which reminded me, I better write it all down, afterward. I didn't want to forget a thing.

"Yes, Lance?" Geez, I surprised myself with a tear in my eye, something that rarely happened.

"Jayma," he repeated.

For fuck's sake, get on with it!

"Sweetie..."

"Yes?" I breathed.

"It's over." He shrugged a little, the way a cashier would when telling you they couldn't give you change for a dollar.

'Course, being the glutton for punishment that I was, I had to have him repeat it.

Which he did. Several times. And then he left.

Dinner was on the stove, warm and ready to be eaten. I was down one boyfriend and down one marriage proposal. So I ate everything.

"OKAY," Shelle said, waiting for me to catch my breath. "Let's think this through. There must be something we can do. Don't give up!"

Easy for her to say. She lived in a house her parents bought her.

"Can't you just sell it?" she asked. "And then pay off the loan?"

"Yes, but that wouldn't cover the entire loan. We overpaid for it, thinking we'd renovate and make a killing."

"Oh, right. Like one of those TV shows where they flip houses," she exclaimed.

"Yeah. Like that. Except it always works out for the people on TV. *My* life is a different story."

"Well. You can come live with me."

That made me cry even harder. "You—you know I'm mildly allergic t—to dogs," I sputtered. "And I have a cat."

"I'll send the dogs to my parents. And I promise to vacuum."

Ugh. What was I going to do?

I was going to get it together, that's what. I wasn't normally one to wallow in my problems. I blew my nose hard and wiped my eyes. Thank god, I didn't wear makeup because by now, it would have run down my face and onto the front of my shirt.

I'd have my little pity party and be done with it. I was going to figure this shit out.

2

CARTER

"Hey, neighbor," I called out to the nice-looking woman next door. What was her name again? Jane something-or-other?

She looked up from where she was crouched by the house's foundation, and waved.

"Hi," she said without much enthusiasm.

I'd had a good day. Was in a good mood. Shit, I felt like talking. I walked over to where she was and squatted down right next to her.

She looked at me with one of those *what the hell do you want?* looks. Damn, I hadn't taken her for such a bitch. But if she wanted to be that way…

I stood back up. "Sorry. Didn't mean to bother you." I headed back toward my house. Christ, the Grinch would have been friendlier.

"Wait," I heard her call. "Hold up."

I turned around.

I'd never really spent any time talking to her and her boyfriend, even though they'd been my neighbors for a couple years. They'd always seemed so…busy. Or uninterested. I was never sure which. What was the guy's name anyway? Larry?

And because they were always on the run, I'd never actually seen her close up. Only from a distance, where I could admire that crazy red hair of hers. And of course, her booming little figure.

Admiring her from afar, I'd not had the chance to appreciate the gorgeous spray of freckles across her face that looked like someone had painted with a tiny pointed brush. They almost didn't look real. And she had brown eyes. People with red hair can have brown eyes?

I thought they had to be blue or something.

Anyway.

"Sorry," she said. "I have a lot on my mind."

"Something wrong with the house?" I asked, pointing at its crumbling foundation.

She sighed. "What *isn't* wrong with this house?"

"Oh. Right. I see what you mean."

Old Man Wagner had lived there since his child-hood. And I think that's the last time anyone spent a cent on the place. Then, this young couple bought it when he died—the redhead and Larry (or whatever his name was). Word in the neighborhood was that they planned to fix it up and sell it for a profit. I hoped they knew what they were getting into.

Renovating a house was not for the faint of heart.

"I'm sorry, but can you tell me what your name is again?" I asked her.

"Jayma. Jayma Kersey." She pointed to the spot she'd been checking out just a minute ago. "This piece of the house here, I think it's called the foundation. It's kind of falling apart. I'm not sure what's wrong with it."

Since her hostility had subsided, I was feeling friendly again.

"Oh, yeah. That's dry rot on the house. And the foundation below it is cracking." Anyone could see that.

But I guess it took her by surprise because she looked like somebody had slapped her.

"Dry rot? Now I'm not exactly sure what that is, but it sounds bad." She shook her head. "Shit."

Whoa. She knew way less about house renovation than I thought she would, considering she was about to get into a big one.

"I mean, it should be something your boyfriend can repair fairly easily."

Her head snapped toward me and she glared. "Um, yeah," was all she said.

Okaaaay…

"I can loan him some tools, if he needs them," I offered. I thought that was pretty neighborly.

"Oh, um, that's okay. He's away. On business."

She bent again to pick at the rotted wood, and I got a glimpse of the top of her thong above her trousers.

God, I was an asshole. The woman had a boyfriend.

If he'd had any sense at all, this boyfriend, he should have been able to fix a little dry rot. On the other hand, whenever I'd seen him, he'd seemed kind of douche-y. Like overly impressed with himself, especially after he found out I was a working class kind of guy. But he was the fool who moved into the money pit with no apparent do-it-yourself skills. He was going to pay through the nose for what he could have learned with little effort. Not that it was my problem.

Me, I was just the contractor next door. Not that he knew that. Because he rarely spoke to me.

"Hey," Jayma turned to me and said, "want to come in for a beer?"

I looked around to make sure she was actually speaking to me.

"Um, sure." I was done working for the day. Why not?

I hadn't been inside the house since long before Wagner had passed, but I sure hadn't been expecting to find what I did.

Chunks of the plaster were missing from the walls, exposing the horizontal lath boards. I knew they'd eventually be replaced with drywall, but a house in that condition could have any number of behind-the-wall problems. Like old electrical, insulation, mold, pests. You name it.

I followed her through what must have been a living room, sidestepping the sawhorse covering a huge hole in the floor. The kitchen looked serviceable, with a 1970's fridge and stove, but the enameled sink looked original, and the linoleum floor was worn in a few spots to the subfloor. I took a look around. Just as I'd remembered it, the house had good bones, but it was in need of some serious TLC. A cat hissed from the corner of the kitchen and took off running.

"Is a Stella okay for you?" she asked, pulling two beers out of the fridge.

Honestly, any sort of beer was okay for me.

"So," I said, taking a long draw on my cold one, "what's your plan with the house? You and your boyfriend, I mean. Hey, what's his name, again?"

Her lips pursed. Christ. Better not ask any more questions about the boyfriend. They must have gotten in a fight or something.

"Lance. His name was Lance. I mean, *is* Lance." She gave a little laugh. Sounded forced, if you asked me.

I took another swig of my Stella. "Oh, that's right. Yeah."

"How long have you lived next door?" she asked.

"'Bout ten years. I knew the last owner of this house, Wagner. He was a great old guy."

She looked around the house. "Maybe, but he sure left this place a mess."

"No kidding," I agreed, looking around. Oh shit, that was rude. "I mean…sorry. Didn't mean to say your house was a mess."

She smiled, her freckles practically jumping off her

cheeks. "It's okay. It *is* kind of a shithole. We had planned—I mean, are planning—to renovate and then sell." She looked at her beer bottle, playing with the label.

Okay, something was definitely up. And I wanted no part of it. I hoped the boyfriend hadn't been a dick to her.

I continued talking. What the hell? I didn't have anywhere to be. "Yeah, I've been in my house ten years and have been a contractor about eleven." I shook my head. It was incredible how fast time had moved.

She tilted her head as she studied me. "How'd you get into your line of work? Had you always enjoyed building things?"

It's funny how life sometimes just happens to you. Or doesn't.

"My dad was a contractor, and I used to help him during the summers and the weekends. When he passed away, I took over to finish up what he had in the works and close out the books. One thing led to another, and ten-plus years flew by."

She stood from her chair. "Hey, I was going to make a little dinner. Would you like to join me?"

"Uh, sure. That sounds nice. Thank you."

She started taking some things out of the fridge. Green beans, chicken, potatoes. Simple, fresh, real— just how I liked it.

But where was Lance?

When her back was to me, I peeked around the

corner of the kitchen, where I could see through the living room into one of the bedrooms. The house was in bad shape, but it was tidy enough.

There were no signs of Lance or any other guy.

Maybe she'd killed him. And stuffed him through the hole in the floor in the living room.

Kidding.

I could help them with their house. Every contractor's dream was to tear something to the studs and build it anew. But my dad had always said to be careful who you do business with and to try to stay away from friends and neighbors. If, god forbid, anything went wrong, there would always be bad blood.

So I came up with another idea.

"Hey, I know a lot of contractors. I could recommend a couple."

She turned from whatever was sizzling on the stove. "*You're* the contractor. Why aren't you suggesting yourself?"

Think fast.

"Oh, um, because I'm pretty much booked. I know lots of other good folks, though." Whew, that was close.

She shrugged. "Eh, it's okay. I don't have the money for it anyway."

What? "You have to have money to reno the house. Unless you can do it yourself, which it doesn't look like you can."

She set the food on the table, and it smelled freaking delicious. 'Course I'd been eating so much takeout, anything fresh would have looked like a gourmet meal. And to sit with this beautiful woman, whose boyfriend was MIA.

Jackpot.

I reminded myself to behave. Part of the reason I'd barely spoken to her the whole time she'd lived there was that she was with that guy.

I wasn't sure I believed the "business trip" story. But I did know I had a thing for this woman, and if the douchebag was stepping aside, I was going to look into stepping inside.

3

JAYMA

I'D NEVER PAID MUCH ATTENTION TO MY NEIGHBOR Carter before, but damn, he was a good-looking guy with his deep dimples and sparkly blue eyes. He'd always seemed friendly enough, but Lance was never into getting to know the neighbors, so I'd just never bothered with any of them, either.

Maybe things would be different now.

It was nice to have company for dinner. The place had been awfully empty lately and even more dumpy than ever with Lance out. Not that I was sorry he was gone. I was only sorry I'd spent part of my life with his lame ass, having let him talk me into putting this mess of a house in my name because he had too much debt from law school. And he'd left me with his cat. Although I did like the cat.

He'd been making seventy-five percent of the monthly payment, and I threw in the other twenty-five.

It was pretty equitable when you looked at both our incomes. Then, he paid the bills from our joint account. Except for when he didn't. Like the last few months, apparently.

And now a handsome neighbor sat across from me at my dining table, instead of Lance. I probably should have been embarrassed to bring him in the house, but it was so obvious it was going to be renovated that it didn't matter what the "before" looked like. Only with the way things were going, there was going to be no "after." The "before" would continue as the status quo. And I'd get kicked out and have to move in with Shelle. And her dogs.

"Thank you for dinner," Carter said, taking his plate to the sink.

The only time Lance took his plate off the table was when I asked him to. Which I had to do all the time.

Carter leaned back against the kitchen sink. "That was a great dinner, thank you. Wanna walk down the street for ice cream?"

"Oh, yeah. Let's do it." Nice, thoughtful.

On the way to the corner store, Carter's hand brushed mine. I couldn't be sure, but it seemed like it might have been on purpose. It had been so long since anyone besides Lance had touched me, it felt strange. Like putting on a new pair of shoes. Foreign. Different. But okay.

Once we were served, we stood outside the shop in that ice cream coma people get where they just lick their cones. The one where they stop talking and just look off in the distance like they've been transported to a better place by their tasty treat.

"Hey. Can I tell you something?" Carter asked.

"Um, yeah. Sure." A drip of chocolate coconut ran down my hand, and I licked it off. *Never waste ice cream.*

"I'd always thought about asking you out, except you had—I mean, *have*—a boyfriend."

What? Shit. Did he know something? Ugh. I didn't want him, or anyone besides Shelle, to know Lance had dumped me. I was just too embarrassed by the whole thing, and explaining what had gone down would have been excruciating. I'd have to do it at some point, but I wasn't ready yet, and besides, this guy was pretty much a stranger anyway.

I stopped licking my cone long enough to look at him. His light brown hair shone in the streetlights. I didn't know the guy from a hole in the wall—I mean, I'd met him before, sort of. But I was beginning to like what I saw.

Good thing it was dark, because I felt my face flushing. "Thank you, Carter. That's sweet." It felt so old-fashioned, to be standing on the curb, eating ice cream under a streetlamp, and have a boy say something nice. It took me away from my worries for a moment.

He looked up at the dark sky. "Yeah, well."

We headed home, and wouldn't you know, his hand brushed mine again, not once, but twice. As if he were testing me.

Could he know Lance was gone? No. No way.

And he certainly didn't know the house was on its way to foreclosure. He couldn't know Lance had skipped the last few payments. Unless he was some sort of mind reader.

This guy might have *thought* he wanted to go out with me, but that's only because he was blissfully unaware of the shit situation I was in the middle of.

We stopped at the end of my driveway, ice cream long gone. Carter stuffed his hands in his pockets and raised his shoulders as if he were stretching.

"I have an early morning. Thank you for dinner," he said, moving his gaze toward me.

Wow. Awkward. But why? I thought to shake his hand but mine was all sticky from the ice cream. Plus, it would just be weird.

"I'm glad you could join me. It was nice getting to know you."

He nodded and just stood there.

"Well, um, Jayma. Would you like to go for a drink sometime?" he asked.

Good grief. Either he's an asshole for hitting on another dude's girl, or he figured out Lance bailed and that I'm sad and lonely.

So I decided to test him.

I raised my eyebrows. "But, you know about my boyfriend, Lance, right?"

"Yeah. What about him?"

He gave me a look that could only be described as seeing right through my bullshit.

Damn.

I looked everywhere but at him while I gathered my response.

"You know, don't you?" I asked.

He just gave me a little smile.

Busted.

"Okay. Lance is not on a business trip. Well, he could be on a business trip, but when he returns, he's not coming home to me." Sadness caused a little strangling sensation in my throat. I had to get inside. I couldn't cry in front of some guy I barely knew.

Carter tilted his head and said, "I know."

I nodded. "You know."

"Yup," he said.

Okay. Wow. Caught in a lie.

"How'd you figure it out?" I asked.

"It wasn't hard. First of all, you invited me over. You wouldn't have done that with someone like Lance in the picture. Second, there were no signs of him in the house."

I looked at the ground for a moment, feeling like an even bigger loser than I'd felt *before* Carter came over to look at my falling-apart house. Wait 'til he found out I was about to be homeless.

"You're a smart guy there, Carter," I said.

He raised his hands in that *what can I say?* gesture.

"But I tell ya what," I continued. "You're my neighbor, and I'm not sure it's a good idea to, you know..." I sputtered, "go out."

"All right. If that's how you feel..." He smiled and shrugged. "Thank you again for dinner. I owe you." He turned to walk up to his own house.

Well, shit.

"Carter," I called.

He turned slowly. I couldn't see much in the dark, but he sure was hot in his baggy work pants.

"Yes."

"Huh?" he asked.

"Yes. Yes, let's go for a drink."

"Oh." He nodded slowly. "Cool. Next Wednesday night?"

"Yeah. That would be great." I watched him walk up to his house and close his front door. His porch light flicked on.

I walked up to my house and went inside. I flicked on my porch light, too.

'Course, it didn't work.

"HEY, GIRL!" Shelle said, flying into the hip Distrikt wine bar like a slightly breathless mess. She grinned at me with her adorable gap-toothed smile and threw me a hug.

"What can I get you?" I asked her.

"Um. Beer. I feel like a beer." She settled onto her stool and turned to face me while I waved the bartender over.

"This is a wine bar, Shelle."

"Right. Right. Wine. White wine," she said, batting her eyes at the bartender. "You pick for me, okay?" she asked him.

She captivated everyone, and this guy was no exception. He pulled several bottles from the cooler, an indication he was going to let her do a little tasting.

He hadn't offered to do that for me.

"So, how's the business?" I asked her.

She took a deep breath and rolled her eyes. "Growing. Like crazy! I think I'll have to hire some helpers." She turned to sample the wines the bartender had poured.

"Oh, this one is good. I'll have the sauv blanc," she told him, and he dutifully poured her a huge glass.

"I got my license and am now a certified dog walker!"

Who knew there was a certification for walking dogs?

"So what does that mean?" I asked. "I guess it's better for the business?"

"Absolutely. First, I get a little break on my insurance."

"You have to have insurance for walking dogs?"

"No. You don't *have* to. But I'm making it one of my competitive advantages."

She'd always had a certain level of ambition.

"That's so awesome, sweetie. I'm really happy for you."

"What about you? Heard from Lance? The asshole. I never liked him, you know," she said. "Mmmm, this wine is really good. Wanna taste?"

Why do people never tell you they don't like your boyfriends until *after* you break up?

"He packed up his shit. He's *gone*. Including his portion of the mortgage payment. Which I cannot cover." Shit, that familiar lump in my throat was back.

Shelle reached for my hand.

"I'm sorry. The whole thing is just so shitty."

"Yeah. I have thirty days to get current on the loan. I thought he'd been making the payments, but he'd stopped a few months ago. Fucker." Damn. The tears began to fall.

Shelle dabbed my face with a bar napkin and handed me another in anticipation of a runny nose.

"Okay, then. What about selling it? I mean, can you make some of the improvements quick enough to get a decent price?"

She had a point. I wondered if anyone would help me with the house and let me pay them after it sold with the proceeds.

"The whole point of buying the house was that we could flip it quickly. There's a lot to be done, and I'm not sure we could do it before the bank comes to take it. But maybe…"

"All right. *Now* we're cooking with gas." She loved sayings like that.

"On a positive note, my neighbor asked me out."

She slapped my thigh.

"Damn! You're not even single a week and look at you with a date." She rolled her eyes.

"Well. I wouldn't say I have a date, per se. I mean, I guess it's a date. If you want to call it that."

"Who's the guy? Have I ever seen him over there?"

"No. I never really knew him until the other day. He's hot as hell, though. Tall, with dimples. Super buff. He's a contractor."

Shelle looked at me like she'd won the lottery.

"*What?* What did you say?"

"Oh, you know, that he's tall. Pretty eyes. Really long eyelashes—"

"No, you idiot. You said he's a *contractor*."

Oh. I get it.

I shook my head hard. "No. Shelle, I can't ask him to work on my house. It would be too weird."

She threw up her hands in exasperation. "Girl, you have a lot on the line here. Use your head. Or maybe another body part."

She threw her head back and laughed with her gap-toothed grin.

4

TANNER

How did I get into such a situation?

I was the only dude in the room. That, in itself, was not a problem. The advertising business had more women than men, generally, so that was business as usual for me.

But to be the only guy in a room of eleven women discussing *tampons*?

Fuck. I did not sign up for this. I mean, did I really need to know which of my coworkers had a heavy monthly flow? Or which ones got sore breasts? Or what size tampons everyone preferred?

I didn't even know they *came* in sizes.

Are you even allowed to talk about shit like this at work, anyway?

But I guess when your client is the world's biggest tampon brand, then period talk was a given. *If you can't stand the heat, then get out of the kitchen,* and all that...

I got a few glances during the meeting, but my presence did nothing to hamper the conversation.

The stuff of my nightmares.

And I'd already asked my boss to take me off the account.

"Marilyn, why do you want a guy working with a tampon client? I mean, what could I possibly contribute?" I asked her.

"First of all, there is nothing wrong with menstruation—"

"I didn't say there was! It's just that since I don't menstruate, I don't see what value I'd be adding to the discussion." Jesus Christ, get me off this fucking account.

"Tanner," she started, using her patient voice that was code for *I'm going to get pissed if you don't back off,* "you are the best media buyer in the company. This client is a huge win for us, and I put together the strongest team we have. A little period talk won't kill you."

She turned back to her computer, code for *this discussion is over.*

I'd worked with her for a long time. I knew her codes.

Shit.

I exited her office, steeling myself for a new life immersed in feminine hygiene products, when a loud voice boomed from the office's reception area, nearby. It wasn't a happy one.

"I told you I needed this done right away," a male voice bellowed.

A subdued female voice responded. I couldn't hear what she was saying, but I had a feeling she was in what they called "a one-down position." You know—powerless. I poked my head into the reception area.

"Hey, guys. All good here?" I asked.

Standing there was Bob, the douchebag from finance, and our receptionist, whose eyes were wide in her bright red face. One might say she looked terrified.

What was her name again?

Bob opened his big trap to start mouthing off again but seemed to think better of it. In a huff, he brushed past me and headed back toward his office.

The receptionist, whose name I suddenly remembered—Jayma—was blowing her nose and dabbing her red eyes.

"What happened, Jayma? Are you okay?"

She sniffled.

"Yes. I'm fine." She shuffled papers around on her desk to avoid looking at me. "I'm really fine. Thank you." She looked up at me. Mmmm, cute with big brown eyes.

"Okay. Okay. I can punch him out for you, if you like. Or just fuck up his email."

She looked at me, brows knit.

And she burst out laughing.

My specialty. Breaking up tension. Making people laugh. Talking about periods.

She took a deep breath. "It's all good. It was just a misunderstanding. Of course, I'm happy to help Bob."

Shit, I don't know why I'd not paid more attention to this woman before. She was fucking gorgeous with her crazy red hair and freckles.

"Jayma?"

"Yes?" she asked brightly.

"I'm Tanner."

"I know you're Tanner," she said.

"Right. Right. How long have you worked here?"

"Um, let's see. Nearly two years."

"Geez. I don't think we've ever had a receptionist stay that long."

"Yeah, well, I'm hoping to have the chance to work on some accounts at some point. You know, move up the ladder."

Cool. She had some ambition.

"You know, I started in the mailroom," I said.

"Yes, I know."

"How do you know that?"

She smiled like she'd been busted. "I guess I've made it a point to learn how all the senior management got to be so successful."

"Tanner?"

I whipped around to see Marilyn.

"Are you joining us in our next meeting? Or do you plan to stay out here and chat all day?"

God, she could be a bitch. She was good at what she

did, but she kicked me in the balls every chance she got.

"Be right there, Marilyn," I called over my shoulder.

I turned back to Jayma, who was trying to keep a smile off her face. I couldn't blame her. I'd laugh, too.

"So, you coming to the work happy hour tonight?" I asked.

She frowned but then immediately brightened up. "Yeah. Yeah I am. Do you know where it is? I can't remember."

"Um. Belden's. It's at Belden's. Well good, then. I gotta run."

"See ya."

I FINALLY HAD a meeting where I was *not* the only man, this time for a client who made automobile air filters. Car parts were about as unsexy as you could get, but it was nice to work on a manly product after two hours of tampon talk. And the cool thing was, the filters were in every car and truck, and when they wore out, they needed replacing. Point being, the market for them was huge, and there was a ton of money to be made. And they'd just hired us to run their ad campaigns.

Smart move on the client's part, if you asked me. Not to brag, but we were good at what we did.

"Tanner? Tanner, are you here with us? Hello?"

It was Marilyn again. Giving me shit. Kicking the old balls. I shifted in my chair, partly to make sure the boys were still there.

"Sorry, Marilyn. Was just thinking about the tampon client from earlier today."

Big lie. But it sounded damn good.

"Anyway…yes, we need to run ads in all the auto-motive magazines and websites…"

WHEN FIVE O'CLOCK HIT, people starting popping their heads into my office.

"Tanner, you coming with?"

"Hey, why are you still at your desk? Let's go."

"Dude, beers on the company. Whatcha waitin' for?"

"I'll be right there. Save me a seat," I yelled after them. I had another email to finish, and then I wanted to see if Jayma was really going like she said she was.

When everyone in the office was gone, I went out to find her, but her spot was empty. She'd either headed out with the rest of the gang or had blown off happy hour.

I took a sec to check out her desk. She had a picture of herself with another woman who had several dogs on leashes. Must have been a friend.

Then something caught my eye. It was a letter from a bank.

Normally, I would never snoop on someone's desk, but this thing was just sitting out in the open, like Jayma had meant to stuff it in her bag and forgot. And I couldn't lie. I read the first couple lines in the letter. It was something about being late on a mortgage payment.

I looked around the office to make sure I was alone, and then turned the paper so I could read it better.

Holy shit. A house that she had a mortgage on was going to be foreclosed because she'd not been making payments. Man that sucked. Left me with a bit of a pit in my stomach. I mean, people need to pay their bills and so forth, but anyone could fall on hard times. And I would not wish something like that on my worst enemy—if I had one.

Okay, so now I felt like total fucking shit for reading this poor woman's letter, which was absolutely none of my damn business. How was I going to look at her now, knowing what I did?

FIVE MINUTES later I walked into Belden's, where happy hour was in full swing. It was a cozy little place with good bar food and cheap happy hour beer, which is probably why the company agreed to spring for a social hour. Who was I to complain?

And I'm embarrassed to admit it, but the moment I

got there, all I wanted to do was see Jayma. My curiosity about the girl who wanted to move up in advertising, but who also owned a house that was being foreclosed on, was ruling the moment.

I mean, how does a receptionist afford a house, anyway?

There was definitely more to what met the eye with this one and my curiosity—not to mention libido—were piqued.

5

JAYMA

JAYMA

Fuckers. I'd known nothing about goddamn happy hour until Tanner spilled the beans when he was nosing around the reception area. I might be the lowly receptionist, but that didn't make it okay to forget to include me in the office social activities.

The nice thing about being annoyed with my coworkers was that it pushed my home problems to the bottom of my worry pile. I could only get upset over one thing at a time. Well, maybe two things. But I wasn't about to make myself more miserable than I already was.

Anyway, so that no one would ever forget to include me again, I was doing my best to be the life of the party. I was making the rounds speaking with everyone from the top executives down to the—well, I was the lowest person on the totem pole. Still, I wormed my way into conversations people were having, chipped in a few witticisms, and was sure to laugh hard when everyone else did. If I was going to move up the ladder, I had to make sure I was on everyone's radar, right?

I spotted the owner and founder of the agency elbowing his way up to the bar for a refill. I dumped the people I was talking to—or should I say listening to, since I didn't have much to contribute anyway—and pushed my way into position next to him.

"Oh, hi, Mr. Renner!" I said, as if he was the last person in the world I thought I might run into that night.

He looked around, and when his gaze settled on me, he seemed confused for a second.

Oh, for heaven's sake. He didn't know who I was. Or maybe he did, but not well enough to place my face when out of the office.

Jerk.

"Hello…" he said, as if he were leaving a blank for me to fill in with my name.

"Jayma. Jayma Kersey," I told him.

"Yes! Jane! Right."

Should I have corrected him? Because I couldn't bring myself to.

Seemed he had nothing else to say.

But that was okay, because I was ready and willing to fill the void.

"Mr. Renner," I said, trying not to stare at what I was pretty sure a bad toupee, "thank you for inviting us all tonight. It's really a lot of fun."

Okay, that was a lie. But it was only wise to thank the person picking up the check, right?

"You're welcome, Jane. I hope you have fun." He looked around, probably for someone he'd rather talk to besides me. Couldn't say I blamed him.

There was a tap on my shoulder. I whipped around to see who it was and gave Mr. Renner the chance to escape that he'd been looking for.

"Hey, Tanner." I wonder if he was going to call me Jane, too.

"Jayma. Cheers." He clinked his glass against mine.

I had to admit, he was adorable in that Clark Kent/Superman sort of way with short, tidy hair, and somewhat nerdy glasses. I could just see the tip of a tattoo peeking out from his shirt collar and several closed up piercings on his ears. Was he a closet bad boy?

Anyhow, I don't know what the hell he was doing talking to me. He'd never paid much attention to me before.

Wait. Maybe he was sensing my tremendous potential?

I clicked into networking mode.

"So, Tanner, I heard you were put on the new account. The tampon one."

He rolled his eyes, then quickly looked around to

make sure no one saw. He lowered his voice. "Yeah, can you fucking believe it? I mean, what do I know about tampons?" He blushed for a moment. Like it hurt to say *tampon*.

Whoa. He was confiding in me. I didn't understand this change in behavior, but I was going to work it.

I looked around too, out of respect for his desire for secrecy. "I know, right. Kind of weird to have a dude working on feminine hygiene products." I figured I could say dude since he so freely dropped the F-bomb.

He pointed to the stool behind me and plopped on one himself. Was he suddenly my buddy?

As I sat, he leaned closer. I looked around to see if anyone was paying attention.

He smelled nice. Kind of like something pine-ish and clean. Hair gel? He looked like he might wear hair gel.

"It was so freaking weird. Listening to my coworkers talk about...you know."

Geez. He couldn't say the word *period*? Well, this was my big chance to help him.

"Look. It's a natural thing. You'll get used to it." I nodded with authority. I mean, I had been getting periods since I was thirteen, so I knew something about the subject.

"Yeah. Well, I hope so." He did not look convinced.

Ugh. Bob from finance had just arrived at the gathering. I looked away quickly so I wouldn't have to say hi.

Tanner waved over the bartender for another round. "So what about you?" He leaned back and studied me.

"Me? What do you mean?" Which part of my sucky life was he inquiring about?

"You know. How's life as a receptionist at an exciting ad agency?"

Was he freaking kidding? I transferred calls, opened mail, kissed asses. Got paid shit.

Stay positive. Smile.

"Oh, well, it's interesting. I mean, I get to meet all sorts of people."

That was sort of true. I saw the mayor one time. Not sure he saw me, though.

"But," I continued, "I'd really like to do some account work."

"That's great. You can't be a receptionist forever. How 'bout this?" he asked. "I can give you a couple things to work on, basic things—nothing big—but we'll see how you like them."

"Oh, wow, that would be great. I'd really appreciate that." Hell, yes.

"Yeah, you know another—"

"Hey, guys," Bob said from behind us. Of course, we turned around.

"Hey," Tanner said.

Bob looked around with an air of excitement. I wondered if he realized he needed to trim his nose hairs? Just imagine how hairy his back would be. Ugh.

"This place is great!" He leaned close enough to breathe on us. "And when the company's paying for drinks, even better!"

He must have had tuna fish for lunch.

"Bob, did you get your stuff straightened out?" I asked him.

Guilt washed over his face.

He looked down at his beer. "Yeah. Yeah, I did. Sorry for being an asshole. I was under a lot of pressure."

Tanner clapped him on the back. "Happens to all of us." He got off his barstool and stood to his full height.

What was that all about?

"And, Bob. Next time I hear you raising your voice to Jayma, or anyone else in the office, you'll have to answer to me."

Dayum, as they say.

I could swear some beer sloshed out of Bob's cup.

"You got it, Tanner." He grimaced and walked away.

Tanner sat back down and pushed his glasses up on his nose. Nothing like a combo badass geek.

"You can't really do anything to him, can you?" I asked as soon as Bob was out of earshot.

He frowned. "No, of course I can't do anything. But he doesn't know that."

Oh my god. This guy was a baller. Definitely wanted him on my team. Or to be on his. Whatever.

And just as I was wondering if he knew how to fix up old, run-down houses, he dropped his bomb.

"Anyway. I was gonna ask you before Bob came over if you'd like to have lunch sometime. You know, sort of like a date."

Oh. Oh my.

Now it was my turn to look around and make sure no one was nearby.

"Um, well. I'm not sure that's such a good idea. I mean, since we work together and all."

But damn, he was awesome. Maybe I could quit and get a job somewhere else and *then* I could have lunch with him. The way he looked at me, like I was really something special, made my heart pound. And forget about how Lance had just walked.

He pursed his lips and nodded slowly. "Yeah, you're probably right. Probably not a good idea. Well then, let's just have lunch as work friends. We can try out that fancy new place down the street."

Darn. I was actually hoping he'd try to convince me there was nothing wrong with dating a coworker. So much for that.

"Yeah, that would be great. I've been dying to go there."

"Okay. We'll do it."

Now it was my turn to ask some questions.

"What about you? How do you like your work at the agency?"

He took a deep breath. "Well, I love it. It's a great job. But my hours are long, and I never seem to get to take a vacation. So that sort of sucks."

He was looking at me like he wanted to say something else. Like he knew me in a way that was impossible considering we'd barely had one conversation, let alone discussed anything meaningful.

I stood up from my barstool. I wanted to get out before the alcohol had me spilling my guts. "Well, I gotta hit the road. It was great talking to you, Tanner. Thank you for the encouragement. It really means a lot."

I wanted to shake his hand, but that seemed ridiculously formal. So, I reached up and gave him a mini-hug. I didn't care if anyone saw. It was way better than a handshake anyway.

6

WYATT

I'D NEVER SEEN SUCH A MESS.

In all the years I'd worked as a plumber, with all the nastiness I'd had to fix, I had never seen a mess like the one that was Deer Plumbing's financials.

On top of that, numbers were not really my strong suit, so that made things even worse. But I was determined to learn. I *had* to learn, now that Dad was in the final stages of Alzheimer's.

I'd been backpacking somewhere on the other side of the world—I can't remember exactly where—when I'd checked email and found an urgent message from my mother. Could I come home?

Was I in Thailand? Or was it Cambodia? Anyway.

I got the first flight home that I could. Dad had fallen and bumped his head. Mom wouldn't usually have called me home for something like that. When you work in the trades like my dad did, you got hurt every once in a while. It was expected.

But he wasn't getting better. They checked him for a brain injury, but all the tests came back negative.

That's when our family doctor found Dad had Alzheimer's.

He was the hub of our family, a real high-quality man, and my biggest supporter. To say it was devastating didn't begin to describe it. I knew the road ahead was not going to be easy. And that included taking over the family business.

I'd tinkered in plumbing for as long as I could remember. But I hadn't intended to do it as a career. After my travels, I'd planned to go back to college.

So much for that.

Now, I was dealing with unpaid tax bills from years gone by. Dad had not really been one to worry about the details. He just wanted to make sure his customers were taken care of. Hell, he didn't really even care if they paid him or not, I realized as I faced a shoebox full of unpaid invoices.

My cell rang, and I saw it was my mother. "Mom."

"Hi, honey. Are you still at work?"

"Yup. Just trying to sort out some of the finances."

"Well, a call came in from a customer. Sounds like an emergency."

"Okay. Text me the number, and I'll call them right away."

Yes. The bookkeeping could wait.

It was a straightforward house call. No hot water.

The poor homeowner... When I told her she was going to need a new hot water heater, she looked like she was going to cry. Although to be honest, almost every time I gave someone news like that, they looked like they were going to cry. Women, men, it didn't matter. No one wanted to spend their hard-earned cash on something as utilitarian as a new hot water heater.

But hey, if you want hot water, you've got to have something to heat it with.

"How much will that be?" Her eyes were hopeful.

I ran my hand through my hair to stall. From the looks of the house, it was pretty darn obvious she was operating on a tight budget. In fact, I was kind of surprised what a dump the place was. What the hell was she doing living there?

Before I could answer, her cell rang.

"Excuse me, one sec, please."

She scurried off, giving me the chance to admire her tight little body and wavy red hair. I'd never been a redhead sort of guy, but she was hot as hell in what I guess were her work clothes—a clingy little dress and some low-cut boots.

I took a second to look around the kitchen. I had to

say, the place had great potential. It would be fun to breathe some life into it.

"Okay, got that taken care of. Now, where were we?" she asked.

Shit, she had the most perfect splay of freckles across her nose. And those dark eyes. Such a contrast against her pale skin.

"Right. Well, a new hot water heater, installed, will run you about fifteen hundred bucks."

She swallowed hard. "Really?" she said in a small voice.

"I'm afraid so. Do you own the place?"

Of course she owned it. No one would rent a place like that.

She nodded. "Yep. It's all on me. No landlord to go to."

The way her shoulders slumped just about killed me.

"I might be able to work on it a bit, see what I can do."

"Really? You could do that? Oh, that would be great." She gestured toward the kitchen sink piled high with dishes.

She must have seen me looking at some fresh cookies sitting on a cooling rack. "Hey, want a couple butter cookies? And I can make you some coffee."

Now, she was talking.

I set to work to find out if there was anything salvageable about the hot water heater. Honestly, it should have been replaced awhile back, but no one ever did that until they were in dire straits. Couldn't say I blamed them. You can do a lot more fun things with fifteen hundred bucks than buy household appliances.

I guessed she didn't have anything else to do, at least not until she had hot water, because she pulled up a stool and started chatting while I worked.

"So, when did you take over for your dad?"

"Um, pretty much in the last year."

"I was sorry to hear about his Alzheimer's. Your mother told me when I called."

I stole a glance at her sympathetic face. God, she was gorgeous.

"Thank you. I hadn't planned on taking over the business from him, but what can you do? Duty calls."

She nodded. "What would you be doing if you hadn't taken it over?"

Boy, I'd spent a lot of time thinking about this one.

"Well, I'd had plans to travel through South America. I'd already spent a bunch of time in Southeast Asia."

"You're a wanderer!"

I took a gulp of the coffee she'd given me. "Yup, I am. I mean, I was. That's all behind me now." I hated the way that sounded. Shit.

"No, no, no. You'll get back out there some day. You're not trapped. *I'm* trapped." She looked down at her hands.

"What do you mean you're trapped?" It was as if a dark cloud had floated over her pretty face.

"Look at this place." She gestured around the room. "I had a boyfriend who was going to help me renovate. And he just bailed."

Shit. Her bottom lip shook and her face turned pink. I hated it when women cried.

"I'm sorry."

She pressed her lips together for a moment. "Yeah. The really shitty thing is that the note for the house is in my name. He split and left me with the bills."

"Goddamn, what a dick."

"No kidding." She smiled sadly.

"What are you going to do?"

"Not sure." She looked down at her hands.

Man, that sucked. What an asshole.

I stood and wiped my hands on my pants. Shit, the place was nothing to look at, but it wouldn't take much to fix it up, either. Just a few bucks and some sweat equity. But I had to stay out of other people's problems. I'd learned that the hard way.

Still…

"Okay," I started, "here's the situation." Hard life lessons be damned. I was going to help this woman if I could.

"The work I did was a bandaid fix. It won't last for long. You *will* need a new hot water heater and pretty soon. What I can do is look around for a used one that's in decent shape. It could buy you a few years 'til you need to spring for a brand-new one."

"Oh, that would be awesome." She clapped her

hands together and jumped up and down. Good grief, she was cute.

"What do I owe you?" she asked.

I waved my hands. "Nothing. Don't worry about it."

Her mouth dropped open, and she shook her head violently. "No, no, no. Please tell me what I owe you for today." She walked over to her wallet and pulled out some bills.

"I'm serious," I said. "You fed me coffee and baked goods. We're even."

""Oh, yeah, those were real high-dollar items." She laughed. "I'm *paying* you. Please let me. I'll feel uncomfortable, otherwise," she insisted.

I had to laugh. "Okay. Twenty bucks. But no more."

She handed me some bills, and we stood there looking at each other. I was pretty sure that was my opening.

"Would you like to go out with me some time?"

Her eyes widened and she studied me. "Do you ask all the ladies with broken hot water heaters out?"

I nodded. "I do. I have a thing for women with bad hot water heaters. They're hot as hell." I guffawed at my punch line. I couldn't help it.

She rolled her eyes, which I totally deserved. "Okay, funny guy. That sounds good. But please keep the plumber jokes to a minimum."

"No promises," I said. "I'll call you tomorrow, then?"

She flipped that crazy red hair back over one of her shoulders. "Okay, sure. And if the hot water heater fails between now and then, I'll be wanting my money back."

"Good one," I said and left. As I walked away, I looked back at the house. It really had potential. And that wasn't the only thing.

7

JAYMA

HOLY SHIT.

Old Mr. Deer had certainly turned out some amazing offspring.

I was trying hard to remember that every cloud had a silver lining. I might have some fucked up plumbing problems, but I'd just been asked out by the best-looking world traveler/plumber I'd ever seen.

Well, okay. I'd never actually met a world traveling plumber, but I'm sure this guy Wyatt was the best-looking one there was.

I'd embarrassed the hell out of myself, though. He'd asked me if the pilot light was on. I said no, it wasn't. Turned out, I had no freaking idea what a pilot light was.

But I did now. He'd shown me.

Initially, he'd been kind of standoffish. Unfriendly. All business. I was fine with that. It's not like I invited him over to hang out and watch a movie. But he changed when I asked him about his father. Warmed right up.

I might be homeless soon, but I had some pretty hot guys to spend time with. Carter the neighbor, Wyatt the traveler. Tanner, from work. When it rained, it poured, as they said.

"SHELLE!" I hollered, running across Alta Plaza Park. Also known as Poop Park. Everyone walked dogs there, and barely anybody picked up after them.

"Hey, slutbag," she hollered back, waving like a maniac. Several heads turned to see what sort of slutbag I was, and then turned back.

"Thanks for screaming that across the park," I told her as I caught my breath.

She waved her free hand in the *no big deal* motion. Her other one held five—no, six—dog leashes. By some miracle, she had all the pups lined up like a row of soldiers, not moving and not barking.

She threw her arms around me in a big hug, tangling us both up in the leashes. She stepped back, beaming her huge gap-toothed grin. Only on Shelle could a space between two front teeth be so attractive.

"You won't believe what happened!" she said.

I'd thought we were getting together to talk about my housing tragedy. Guess not. At least not yet.

"A client asked me out…" she sang, jumping up and down.

"Oh, that's awesome, sweetie." Actually, she got asked out all the time. But I was still happy for her.

She nodded. "Yup. He lives in this big house in Pac Heights and has the coolest Labradoodle. I can't wait," she squealed.

We walked over to a park bench and sat for a moment. Couldn't rest for long with the dogs. After all, she was paid to *walk* them, not sit around with them.

"And, San Francisco Magazine is doing a 'Best Of' issue. I'm going to get all my friends, family, and clients to vote me the city's best dog walker."

"Oh, what a great idea. You have my vote. Do you get anything if you win?"

She shook her head. "Only tons of free publicity! There's nothing more I could possibly want."

"So. My house." I clearly needed to steer the conversation.

"Yes. Let's talk about the house," she said, nodding.

"I'm thinking if I could get some work done really quick and tell the bank I'm going to sell, they may give me more time before they foreclose. It would be better for them because they'd get their money, and better for me because it would save my credit rating and give me a place to live awhile longer."

She shrugged. "I guess you could always ask."

"Right. If it means the bank is getting its money, you'd think they'd work with me." My logic hadn't always succeeded. I'd also thought Lance would be with me through the renovations, and possibly marriage. And look what happened with all that.

Shelle stood. Time to get moving. The dogs had started falling asleep. She gave their leashes a little tug and they all popped up, following us out of the park and down the street.

"Hey, now. Don't be upset. You'll figure it out," she said.

"I know. I know." I searched my pockets for a tissue. "I just don't get how Lance could have screwed me over like this. I hate him. I fucking hate him. And that slut at his office. I mean, we went to Christmas parties at her house."

"Fucking bitch," she added in solidarity, patting my back. "Now what's the plan? Where do we start?"

"I don't know. I mean, I have some ideas. Still trying to figure it out. But—I do have some good news. The plumber who came by the other day, who was wicked good-looking, asked me out."

"No way! Everyone's asking you out lately," she said.

"It's weird, isn't it? I guess they can smell I'm lonely and broken-hearted."

"Jayma! Hey, Jayma!" a voice called from a distance.

"Who's that?" I asked, looking around. On the other side of the street, someone was waving his arms.

Holy shit. It was Tanner.

"Oh my god. I know that guy from work," I said.

"Whoa. You know *that* guy? Shit. I've seen him jogging before. I nearly stepped in front of oncoming traffic just staring at him," Shelle whispered.

He ran across the street toward us. With his T-shirt tucked into the waistband of his workout shorts.

Oh. My. God. He had no shirt on.

And you know that tattoo I thought I saw poking out of his collar?

It was a long string of musical notes. Was he a secret rocker?

That would be seriously hot.

I had to force myself to look up at his face and not his defined pecs, nor his perfectly flat stomach. It was torture.

Shelle apparently felt the same way. She extended her hand without hesitation.

"I'm Shelle, Jayma's friend."

"Oh, hi. I'm Tanner, also Jayma's friend. From work, that is," he said, looking at me. He was missing her batting eyelashes, but that didn't stop her from trying.

"Tanner. What a surprise. You live around here?" I asked.

"Yup. Just a couple blocks over that way," he said, pointing up a steep hill. No wonder he was in such good shape. "So what are you two up to?"

I shrugged. "Just taking a walk. Shelle has a dog walking business. I joined her on the walk so we could catch up." Why was I babbling? All that was pretty obvious.

Just then, one of the dogs in Shelle's care took a big crap on the sidewalk. Tanner and I took a step away, and Shelle started rooting through her pockets for a plastic bag, dignity all but gone, as well as any interest in my handsome colleague.

"So, I'll see you at work tomorrow, yeah?" he said.

"Oh, yeah. I'll be there. See ya."

While Shelle was still struggling with dog shit—maybe they didn't teach poop handling in the certification class—I watched him walk away. As he got to the bottom of the hill he'd pointed toward, he started *jogging* up it. Not walking, but jogging.

Who the hell *runs* up a hill?

8

DIG

MY BUDDY CARTER HAD SOMEONE HE WANTED ME TO meet.

I knew what that meant. The question was, did she want to meet me?

We were kind of quiet about our particular procliv-ities. Not that we had anything to hide, and not that we were ashamed. It's just that not everyone was as open-minded as we'd like them to be. But, hey, we were in San Francisco, where almost anything could go. Almost.

We liked to date one woman.

That is, one woman between the two of us. You know, like, share.

We hadn't dated anyone in a while, but we were feeling ready. We didn't talk about it much—it was just something we *knew*. And when he told me about his adorable, newly single red-haired neighbor, I was all over it. If Carter said she was a sweetie, that was good enough for me. He had very high standards. I was the happy beneficiary of that.

I was headed over to meet the two of them for happy hour at some little joint downtown. It had taken me forever to get out of the office, and I was late, thanks to clients. Turns out, if your marriage is on the rocks and you're fighting like cats and dogs, then buying a home is not going to fix things. But you can't say that to clients.

Go figure.

They—well, the wife—was pregnant, on top of everything else. Another attempt to save the marriage, I suppose. But they'd signed on the dotted line and written a giant down payment check. They'd get the keys to their new home soon, and I wouldn't have to listen to them fight again.

Well, until they split up and had to sell the house. They'd call me for that. I just knew it.

I spotted Carter right off the bat when I arrived. The woman he was with had her back to me, so I couldn't see her, but he was right about her hair. Long, thick red waves I wouldn't have minded burying my face in. And if I played my cards right, maybe I'd get to.

"Hello," I said, clapping Carter on the back and extending my hand to the beauty before me.

As soon as we touched, I knew. I knew I had to know this woman better, but that I also needed to take my time with her. One glance at Carter, and it was clear we were on the same page.

She looked up at me with dark brown eyes and smiled. "Hi. I'm Jayma."

"Nice to meet you. I'm Dig," I said, grabbing a barstool and pulling it up to join them. "Sorry I'm late, guys. I had a client issue."

"What kind of work do you do, Dig?" God, she had the most amazing freckles splattered across her face.

"I sell real estate, and I currently have a fighting couple as clients. Good times. What about you?"

Carter sipped his beer and smiled, watching us.

"I work for an ad agency. I'm the receptionist right now, but I hope to move into working with clients soon. It's a pretty cool place."

"Nice." I turned to Carter. "And how was *your* day, my friend?"

He nodded, looking from Jayma to me. "It was okay. Bid on some new jobs and made some progress on hiring more help. Usual stuff."

I turned to Jayma. "I've known Carter and his family nearly all my life. His parents treated me like I was their own when some bad stuff went down with my own family."

Her face lit up. "Oh, you guys are old friends. Like brothers, I guess."

Oh yeah.

"We go way back," I said. "Been through a lot

together. And we hiked the entire Pacific Rim Trail when we were eighteen and came back alive."

Carter laughed. "I hated to come home, but Dig made me. He couldn't hang."

"I don't think so, brother." I turned to Jayma. "Some of us just are not cut out for camping."

Carter nodded. "Some of us are wimps."

I rolled my eyes and laughed. "Anyway, Carter told me you have a little fixer-upper," I said.

"Yeah. It's a fixer-upper, all right. Although, I'm not sure how fixed-up it's going to get. It was a project my boyfriend and I were working on. I may have to default on the loan." Her eyes weren't quite as bright as they'd been a minute ago.

"Default? No way. There must be something you can do. What about selling it?" I suggested.

"I wish. I'm under water on it. I owe more than I can get for it right now. The plan was to fix it up and make a killing. But that does not seem to be happening now." She took a draw on her beer.

I looked at Carter and could tell he was pretty much thinking the same I was.

"You know, since I work in real estate, I might be able to help you with some options," I said.

"Oh, thank you. That's okay, but thank you."

"So what needs to be done with the house anyway?" I asked.

She let out a long sigh and laughed. "How much time do you have? No, really, it's a long list. It needs to be taken down to the studs in some rooms, new electrical, some plumbing. New kitchen and bathroom."

"Whoa. Jesus," I said.

"I've seen the house," Carter chimed in. "It has great bones. Really awesome potential. It's a shame the last owner let it go like he did. But it's nothing that some hard work can't fix."

"Well, there you go," I said to her.

"I'm sure you're right about that." She glanced at her watch. "Guys, I hate to break up a g party, but I have to get back to the office for a bit more work. I'll see you both in the neighborhood?"

We said our goodbyes, and she was gone.

"Damn, buddy. That's one woman I'd like to spend a bunch of time with," I said.

Seriously. I hadn't realized exactly how cute she was until she was walking out the door. Tight skirt hugging her little butt, white blouse with the collar turned up, and some spike-heeled boots. She caught me staring when she looked back over her shoulder just before letting the door close behind her. I was busted.

I didn't care.

I wanted her to know I was interested.

"I feel the same way. We have a date set up for next week," Carter said.

"I know you're looking forward to that, buddy."

"I am," he said, nodding. "I am."

"So tell me. What's the house really like?"

"Well, it's a shithole at the moment. But, like I said,

it would be a pretty straightforward job. Nothing too complicated. Really basic stuff."

"The stuff you do every day, right?"

"Yup."

"Then, what are you waiting for?"

He shrugged. "I'm not sure she wants my help. She seems kind of proud. And I tell ya, that boyfriend she had. What a douche. Totally had his head up his ass. Always acted like he was better than other people. Including her."

"Well, he was obviously an idiot. Who would let someone like her go? I sure as hell wouldn't. You think she'll be interested in our unique arrangement?"

"Dunno."

"Well, I guess there's only one way to find out."

Carter nodded. "And I think we'll know pretty soon."

"I'm looking forward to it," I said.

My phone vibrated in my pocket, and as much as I wanted to ignore it and just enjoy my beer, I reached for it. Real estate was not a nine-to-five job. I had to be ready to deal with clients pretty much around the clock.

"Oh Christ," I said, looking at the caller ID. "It's the fighting couple. I gotta go, man."

I threw some money on the bar, and even though Carter tried to give it back to me, I wouldn't let him. He was always looking out for me.

In more ways than one.

63

9

JAYMA

JAYMA

JAYMA

"Hey!" Shelle hollered, running toward me with five dogs in tow. One of the smaller ones somehow got under her feet, but she righted herself just before wiping out.

Who knew the life of a dog walker was so dangerous?

"Ohmygod, you won't believe it but one of the dogs I was watching got away yesterday. He ran and I couldn't catch up, not with all the other dogs I had. Turned out, he was rounded up by animal control, and I had to go fetch him before the owners found out he'd gotten away."

"Good grief," I said.

"I know, right. Disaster averted. Barely."

We headed toward the Marina Green, one of the

best dog walking places in the city. It was also one of the best places for guy-watching, and guy-meeting. Which was why Shelle liked it so much.

"Hey, what happened to the client who asked you out?" I asked.

"Oh. I haven't told you about him? He chewed with his mouth open." She shook her head.

God forbid.

"No second chances?"

"No. Absolutely not. I can't teach a grown man table manners. His mother should have done that."

She had a point.

"So, I spoke to someone at the bank," I said.

Her eyes widened. "No! You did not! What did they say? What did you say? Tell me everything."

"So I asked them if I could have some more time."

"Yeah? What happened?"

"The guy I spoke to was a total dick. Said that since I was behind in my payments, he had no authority to change what was already underway." I felt that damn lump in my throat return. I was getting tired of crying over this shit.

"No way. God, I'm so sorry to hear that. Is there anything else you can do? Can you talk to their super-visor?" she asked.

"I could try, I suppose. Sometimes, I think those fucking banks just want you to fail. Like they get their kicks out of it. I hate banks."

"I hear ya. Can't live with them. Can't live without

them," she said, nodding. Her phone rang, and she handed me the dog leashes while she fished through her pockets.

"Oh shit. It's the open-mouthed chewer. I'm not gonna answer it," she said.

I rolled my eyes.

"Answer the damn phone. He's nice enough to call you, you be nice enough to answer."

"What?" Clearly, being nice was not part of the equation for her.

"C'mon. Be a nice girl."

She rolled her eyes and swiped her phone *open*.

"Hello?" she said, walking a few steps away from me.

I started walking the dogs to keep them moving when I froze.

It was Lance. Fucking Lance.

With his whore.

I started in the other direction so I wouldn't have to contend with them, when I stopped. What was I running away from?

I tightened my hand on the dog leashes and walked toward the two of them.

"Hey!" I yelled.

They turned around to see who was calling them. Problem was, a lot of other people turned around, too.

Fuck it. I was pissed.

"Hey asshole! Yeah, you, Lance!"

His face was deathly white when he realized I was

the one calling him. He looked around, most likely for a place to hide.

"Thanks to you," I said, pointing in his face, "and your whore here, my house is being foreclosed on, my credit is going to be shit, and I will have no place to live."

The whore screwed up her face like she wanted to take me out. If only she'd lay a hand on me. It would be the perfect excused to slap her Botoxed mug.

Lance held up his hands like he could diffuse the situation. But I kept going.

"I hope you're proud of yourself, fucking me over like you did!" I screamed.

He looked at his whore, grabbed her hand, and starting hustling away.

While I'd been scolding him, the dogs had gathered around my feet protectively. The problem was that when I took a step toward chasing after Lance, my feet were tangled in the leashes. After teetering back and forth trying to catch my balance, I fell on my ass with a *thump*.

Shelle came running up to me and pulled me back to standing.

But she wasn't going to drop things.

"Yeah, run away, you fucker!" she screamed after them. "Chicken shit!"

She was a true friend.

"Are you okay? Sorry about the dogs. Sometimes

they do that." She looked down at them, wagging her finger. They just stared back.

"Okay. Let's keep moving," she said. "I gotta get these guys some exercise so when they go home, they're good and tired."

IT WAS FUNNY, but ever since Tanner had straightened out Bob the accountant, my life at the agency had gotten better. Bob was off my back, and Tanner was making sure to tell me about his accounts when he had the time, so I could really learn more about the business.

"So, how's your day going?" he asked, having stopped by my desk. He was wearing a really hip suit with skinny legs and his shirt was open at the neck. I loved guys in suits with no ties. It made them look like they were doing the walk of shame. Like they'd had a big night partying and had lost their tie somewhere along the way.

"Good. Good. Yours?" I asked in return.

He nodded slowly. "Eh. I'm about to go into another one of those tampon meetings. Last one I was in, I thought I was going to throw up. You wouldn't believe the personal shit the women were discussing. I'll never look at any of them the same way again."

I had to bite my tongue not to laugh. I felt for the

guy. I really did. But c'mon. Was hearing about periods *that* bad? I mean, it was his freaking job. And he was paid pretty well to do it, from what I knew.

"So, hey," he said. "I know you didn't want to go on a quote unquote *date*." He did the air quotes thing with his fingers. "But let's schedule that lunch, okay? As friends, of course."

"Yeah. Let's do that."

As soon as he left the reception area, I called Shelle.

"Yo," I said.

"Whassup, bitch?" she answered.

"So you know the cute guy we saw jogging last week?" I asked.

"The one who works in your office? HELL yes, I remember him. Do you think I'm an idiot?"

I was glad she couldn't see me roll my eyes.

"Yes. That one. Well, we're going to lunch."

"Get. Out. I thought you didn't want to go."

"Well, we're just going as friends."

Big sigh. "Well, if you didn't go, I couldn't be your friend anymore."

Sometimes, I wished she would just shut up and listen. "I just don't think it's a good idea to date anyone from work—"

"You're popular lately."

"I don't know about that. But I am getting asked out. Which will be some nice rebound fun. Thing is, I feel kind of weird going out with these different guys. I mean, it's the only way to get to know them." I lowered my voice. Several company execs went flying out the door, presumably to an important meeting. They took no notice of me, but I still couldn't take a chance on them hearing about my pathetic life.

I continued, "I'm not sure what to do. I mean, go out with three guys? It feels…weird."

I heard dogs barking in the background. "For god's sake. Get over yourself. Just fucking go out with them and stop whining."

"Really? I mean, I don't know."

"Look." She sighed impatiently. "Go out with them all. It's the only way to find out which one you like. See which one is best in the sack. See which one eats the best pussy."

"What? Oh my god, shut up. No way. I can't sleep with them all—"

"Jayma, you were with Lance a long time. Too long, if you ask me. You need to sow some wild oats."

She sure loved saying that.

"And if you have any leftovers, you can send them my way."

What was the harm? It's not like I was going to marry any of them, and besides, I'd be homeless in a month anyway. Might as well have fun before I was a complete and total loser.

CARTER

I HAD TO ADMIT, I'D BEEN LOOKING FORWARD TO SEEING Jayma all day. It had been a long time since I'd looked forward to much of anything, much less a date with a hot freaking redhead. Just thinking about it left my cock twitching.

I felt bad about the situation with her house, and of course, I'd do what I could if she let me. She was proud, not to mention stubborn. But I was certainly happy that douchebag boyfriend was out of the picture. Good riddance to that pretentious ass. I'd never had a good feeling about him, but had absolutely zero respect for him since he'd left Jayma. What a dumbass.

I looked out my window, over at her house, which was the kind of place kids would run by on Halloween, not daring to set foot on the property much less ring the bell and wait for candy. Paint was peeling from the exterior of the house, and the only window I could see that wasn't covered by an old sheet had a long crack through it. Wonder how long that'd been there? She was in a mess of a situation, to be sure, but she was clearly smart and scrappy. She'd find her way out—with or without me—but I hoped *with* me.

I walked across our yards and climbed the rickety steps to her front door. When I rang the bell, she answered almost instantly. Damn did she look cute.

"Ready?" I asked her.

"Yeah! Let me get my keys."

She popped out the door, pulling it shut behind her.

"Let's do it," she said, looking up at me with those brown eyes. She pulled the mass of red hair off her face, securing it with an elastic band she pulled from her wrist.

"Just tell me if you need a little break," I said.

We set off jogging. It had been her idea to get some exercise. I guess she'd seen me on my regular runs and thought I might be able to help her get back into a fitness routine. Of course, I was more than happy to oblige, and I let her set the pace.

As we reached the end of the block, I figured I'd see if she was too winded to talk.

"So when was the last time you ran?" I asked.

"Oh, let's see. I think it's been a couple years. So, I'm basically starting all over."

We went a few more blocks—we had only aimed to do a mile, if she could do that much—when she started breathing hard. She must have been sweating a little too, because I could smell her perfume or lotion or something. Very nice—fresh and clean, just how I liked my women.

I glanced down at her as we approached the end of our mile, and good for her, she was working her ass off. Her face was in a grimace, and she was trying so hard she was oblivious to everything around her, including me. Which was fine, because I could look out for her.

But she didn't pass out, and in fact, finished her mile. She was panting and sweating, and her face was beet red, but she did it, and I thought that was hot as hell.

"How're you feeling?" I asked.

"Um…good…" She was still huffing and puffing. "Got a little cramp in my side, but I'll be okay."

She stopped to try to stretch it out. Wisps of her hair had worked their way out of her ponytail and were sticking to her perspiring face. Several fingers dug into her cramped side.

"Here. I'll help you with that. Take long, slow breaths." I stood behind her. "Place my hand where the cramp is."

"Right…here," she said, pressing my fingers into her side.

It felt damn good to get my hands on her hot little body, even if the intention was to help her stop cramping. And I don't think she minded, either. She leaned into me, continuing with her slow breathing.

"Feeling better?" I asked, my face nuzzled into her moist neck. She smelled like clean girl sweat. Goddamn.

"Yeah…" she said in a breathy voice. "Yeah, that's nice."

Okay. Apparently, that was all I needed. Don't you know, my damn cock was already standing at attention. I backed up so it wouldn't be pressing into her ass. I didn't want to scare her off or send her running the rest of the way home. Even though she looked pretty exhausted and probably couldn't have run another step.

"Can you walk? Ready to head home?" I asked.

She nodded. "Yeah. Let's get back."

I removed my hand from her waist but kept one arm draped around her shoulder while we walked the last couple blocks. She leaned into me just enough to let me know she was into it, and of course, to give me nasty ideas about what I might like to do to her later.

"Oh my god, that smells amazing," she said when we arrived at my place. I couldn't cook many dishes, but I had a chicken roasting. It was one recipe I'd mastered, so I made it over and over.

"It's my specialty," I said with a laugh.

"And what an amazing house," she said, looking around as I led her to the kitchen. She stopped to study some photos hanging in the hallway and then hustled to catch up to me in the kitchen.

"Wine?" I offered.

"Of course. Thank you," she said, accepting a glass. "I hope I didn't ruin your workout by limiting you to a measly one mile run."

"Not at all. I had already run this morning to get my five miles in."

She rolled her eyes. "So you know I'd be lame?"

"No. You'd told me you hadn't run in a couple years, so I knew you'd be limited to a mile or so."

"Well, you were right," she said, pulling up a stool to my kitchen counter.

"You know…" I said, stopping mid-sentence.

She took a sip of her wine. "What? What do I know?"

Oh, what the fuck.

I took a deep breath. "I had a crush on you for the longest time. Even though I hardly knew you." There. It was out.

She turned an adorable shade of pink that turned to bright red. She opened her mouth, but nothing came out. She just looked at her wine, swirling it in her glass, with little bits of hair now dried to her forehead. Shit, I didn't know if I could wait until after dinner to make my move.

I pulled the chicken out of the oven to let it sit before carving it up. When I turned around, she was standing behind me. Right behind me. Close behind me.

I'd always had a weakness for women who took the bull by the horns. So to speak.

One corner of her mouth turned up into the cutest crooked grin I'd ever seen. I ran my finger over her temple to push away her errant strands of hair, and she closed her eyes at my touch.

Not that I wanted to, but there was just no stopping this. I'd wanted her since I first saw her moving boxes into her house with her douchebag boyfriend, although I'd never imagined he'd be fool enough to leave her. His loss, my gain. And, hopefully Dig's, too.

I reached to loosen her ponytail. I had to get my hands in that red hair, and when I did, my heart hammered against my chest so damn hard, I was sure she felt it. She was the perfect package—beautiful, slim, smart, ambitious, and even a little crazy. She did, after all, take on a piece of shit run down old house that most people would have run away from, screaming.

If I didn't watch myself, I'd be down on one knee proposing within the week.

I slowly backed her up to the kitchen counter and leaned to taste those sweet lips, the ones I'd been unable to take my eyes off every time she moved them to speak.

A small growl escaped my throat. She might as well have known how badly I wanted her.

11

____

JAYMA

OH MY. I HADN'T BEEN TOUCHED BY ANYONE BUT LANCE the asshole in several years. And how did it feel to be touched by someone new?

Fucking amazing.

He made me feel...safe. Yeah. I'd not felt safe in a long time.

Sure, Lance had a fancy law degree and a job at a fancy law firm. But he was also insecure and paranoid as hell, always sure someone at work was going to best him, or some guy would try to steal me away from him. That his dick wasn't big enough, or that his back waxer missed a spot. Such a sad way to go through life.

Carter was so...strong and self-assured. That's what it was. He seemed like he'd never be afraid of anything. Like if something bad came his way, he'd find a way to handle it. I needed someone like that on my side.

A huge part of me knew it wasn't a good idea. That

nothing good could come of making out with my hot neighbor. I could have walked out. Said goodnight, thanks for the jog, enjoy the chicken on your own.

But the wine and the nice rock 'n' roll music playing in the background convinced me otherwise—not to mention his hands, which started in my hair and worked their way down the sides of my face to my neck and around my shoulders. One landed on the back of my head and the other on my upper back. Perfect leverage for him to pull me in, which I willingly allowed him to do.

Hell, if he hadn't, I'd probably have thrown myself at him anyway. That's how good it felt to be the object of his attention.

He took a step back to look at me, and I could swear I saw something pass over his eyes. I wasn't sure I could describe it, other than to say there was a passion in them that made me weak in the knees. He returned his mouth to mine with a crash, and I fell right into him as some sort of current washed over me, landing right in my core.

My throbbing core. Damn, it had been a while since I'd felt something like that.

His tongue probed at my lips, gently teasing them apart. He knew where he wanted to go but was willing to wait for me to follow along.

I loved that. No disgusting *shove his tongue down your throat* action.

How could any guy think that's hot anyway? I'd never understood it.

"What about the chicken?" I asked.

He looked over his shoulder at it.

"Are you worried about it?" he asked with a small grin. "'Cause it doesn't look like it's going anywhere to me."

I had to laugh at that.

His hands ran down the back of my workout leggings 'til his fingers reached the cheeks of my ass. With a tight hold, he lifted, plopping me on the edge of the counter. He parted my knees and moved between them, returning to our kiss and wrapping my legs around his waist. My entire body tingled with heat, and through the thin fabric of my workout clothes, I could feel his hard cock.

His kisses moved to my neck when I felt his fingers tease under the hem of my T-shirt. They travelled until they met my sports bra, where he ran his fingers over my nipples, already standing at attention. A slight moan escaped me, and he pulled up my bra until the girls were free. He lifted my shirt over my head and pushed my aching tits together and to his mouth.

Fuck, yeah.

He sucked one and pinched the other, then switched sides, driving me mad with the sensation of pleasure and pain. I leaned back onto the counter with my hands behind me, my head falling back, giving him all the access he needed to make me feel so fucking good, I thought I might cry.

"How you doin', baby?" he murmured.

"Good..." I whispered. "So good..."

"Yeah? You mind if I have a little taste of your pussy?" he growled.

Holy shit, if I hadn't been sitting on my ass, I would have fallen over. I had to nod in agreement, because I couldn't say a fucking word. He helped me down from the counter. I kicked off my sneakers, and he lowered my leggings until I'd pulled my feet out of them. All he left behind were my pink panties and little footie socks.

This time, he lifted me and brought me to the sofa in his living room. But instead of sitting, we walked around to the back of it, where he bent me forward. I gripped the soft cushions on the sofa as he positioned my ass up high and spread my legs as far apart as he could.

I didn't know what the hell he was doing, and I didn't care.

While positioned behind me, he whispered his fingers over my throbbing core, with only the lace of my panties keeping him away from my searing flesh. I wiggled into his touch to increase his pressure and to also let him know I wanted more. Yeah, more.

His fingers hooked into the waistband of my panties and with agonizing slowness, he brought my legs back together to peel them off my ass, down past my thighs, and over my feet. He pushed my legs apart once again, exposing my most private parts. A soft groaned sounded behind me.

It was nasty, and naughty, and I loved it.

His hands smoothed over my ass, when he pried me open to reach my pussy and tongued me from clit to ass and back.

Carter's finger then pushed into my slit. I nearly screamed as he curled it inside me in a *come here* motion. While he did that, I felt his lips on my ass cheeks where he planted tiny little kisses that got closer and closer to my...*Wow*. He was really going there. Oh. My. God.

His tongue tickled my ass—yes, my ass. And I couldn't believe how fucking great it felt. One finger in my pussy, and his tongue on my ass. How come I never knew about this before?

From my inverted position, I dug my hands into the sofa cushions for the leverage I needed to buck my hips in time to his strokes. My nipples got rock-hard, and my entire body broke out in goose bumps. My breath rasped, and my whimpering grew. I was in a goddamn mind-blowing free fall. He pressed harder until my asshole opened just a little for his tongue. I screamed.

An orgasm I didn't see coming hit me like a truck.

My head thrashed, and I could only guess that all the noise in the room was coming from me. I slapped my hands against the sofa cushions while he continued to work my backside and finger fuck me at the same time. He was relentless, dragging me through my orgasm until I thought I might pass out.

When I stopped thrashing, he pulled me to standing, holding me in support against my shaking legs, wrapping his arms around me from behind.

"How you feeling, gorgeous?" he asked.

"Goo…ood. Yeah…good." As my senses came back, I rotated in his arms to face him. I looked up to his sparkling eyes, and he smiled at me, showing off those damn dimples.

"Do you…do you have a condom?" I sputtered. I wasn't done with this guy yet. Not by a long shot.

I was being a hussy. Making up for lost time. Shelle would be proud.

"Yeah, baby." He sat me on the sofa and disappeared for a minute. When he returned, he stood before me, still wearing clothes. I was the only one naked, except for my socks. I stood to pull his shirt over his head, and when I did, holy shit—that guy been hiding some muscles from me and all the women of the world.

I hooked my thumbs in the waistband of his jogging pants. He raised his arms out to the sides as high as his shoulders and closed his eyes. I guessed that was his way of saying *do what you want with me.*

And I planned to.

I lowered his pants and boxers until they fell in a puddle around his feet. His erect cock bounced against my tummy, but I didn't look. I wanted to watch his beautiful face. I reached for his hard-on and found my hand would not even wrap all the way around it. Jesus, and I was about to fuck that monster?

He took my hand and pulled me up, taking the seat on the sofa I had just occupied. In a split second, he had the condom open, rolling it over his erection. He placed his hands on my hips and pulled me forward, putting one of my knees on either side of him. His cock hovered just under my opening. He was in no hurry.

"You have such great tits, Jayma," he murmured, taking turns kissing them.

Then he stopped and looked at me. "Ready?"

I answered only with my smile.

One of his hands held his cock still, and with the other, his fingers gently pried me open. I felt pressure at my opening, and bounced lightly on him while I got used to his girth. He was fucking huge, stretching me to capacity, and then stretching me some more. He rocked his hips to get more deeply inside me, and I threw my head back and moaned.

I had no idea what I was doing with this gorgeous neighbor of mine. But there'd be time to worry about that later.

Right now, I wanted to get *fucked*.

And I was about to be. Seriously.

Carter rocked his hips up toward my opening, this time, burying the remaining thick inches of his cock. We both cried out, his dick filling me perfectly. I was so wet I could feel myself spilling on him, my juices running down his balls and probably to the sofa underneath.

Nothing a little soap and water wouldn't cure.

"Come for me," he growled. "Come, baby. I want to feel you squeeze my cock with your tight little pussy." His muscles clenched and he gripped my ass with his strong hands, pistoning me up and down his length until his jaw tightened and his face turned into a grimace.

He drove into me over and over. One last time, and he swelled inside me even bigger. I screamed again, an orgasm sending white heat through my body, leaving every nerve on fire. He joined me by roaring through his release, pumping me a couple more times until we collapsed into each other, both gasping for breath, and loving our temporary escape from the real world.

"Fuck, baby," he muttered, running his hands through the mess that was my hair.

"Hey, Carter?" I asked.

"Yeah, Jayma?"

"I'm starving. Is that chicken still available?"

12

TANNER

I was hoping Jayma had been smiling all morning because she was looking forward to our lunch. Or maybe there was another reason, like the foreclosure on her house—which she had no idea I knew about— had been resolved in her favor.

Whatever it was, she was glowing with some kind of happiness, which boded well for our time together.

I swung by her desk to say hi after my latest tampon meeting. I needed something to take my mind off my coworkers' cycles. Ugh.

She was on the phone when I entered the lobby, probably taking a message from one of my clients—they called constantly. I glanced down at the place where that letter had been, the one about her foreclosure, but it had been put away somewhere, out of view of nosy people like myself. She peeked up at me from her call and smiled, that adorable spray of freckles coming to life, just like her sparkly brown eyes. Raising one finger in the *wait a moment gesture*, she turned back to her call, typing a message into her PC before clicking her headset to *off*.

"Well, look who it is," she said with her sly grin. Shit, she just killed me. She flipped that red hair back over her shoulder, and I felt a twitch in my pants. I could not deny it. I had jacked myself twice thinking of how I hoped I'd get to grab that hair one day, and hold on for the—

"Tanner? Tanner, are you all right?" She wore a confused look on her face.

"Oh! Yeah. Yeah, I'm great. Sorry, my mind was wandering, thinking about…um, work. You know how that is." Christ. Down, boy.

"So, lunch. I cannot wait—" she started, just as the phone rang again. She mouthed *I'm sorry* and turned back to her computer, ready to type whatever the caller had to say. I slunk back to my desk.

Finally, at noon, I peeked around the corner into my boss Marilyn's office. Papers were spread all over her desk. Clearly, she was up to her neck in something. I scooted past her door before she could see me and call me in to talk.

I had to do that sometimes.

Jayma was standing by the office's front door with her bag in hand and an intern sitting in her spot to handle calls. When she saw me, her face lit up.

Damn, I liked that.

"Okay. Let's go," I said. We were just going out to lunch as friends, so there was no need to worry about any office gossip.

Regardless, I'd made a reservation at the restaurant we'd discussed, a happening place not far from the office, famous for being in one of the oldest buildings in all of San Francisco. It was stunning, with exposed brick and lots of heavy wood trim.

"Oh my gosh. I have wanted to come here for so long. This is awesome," Jayma said as I held the door for her.

She followed the hostess to our seats, providing me the opportunity to walk behind her and admire her slim black skirt and sky-high fuck me pumps. Made me glad I was wearing a suit jacket to hide, my um...admiration.

"This menu looks delish," Jayma said as she looked up just in time to see several plates of food go by.

She set her menu aside and gave her order to the waiter.

"So," she said.

"Yes?" I said. Seemed she had something on her mind.

There was that goddamn smile again. And the freckles...

"Do you ever do anything besides work?"

This is what she had on her mind?

"I fit in some exercise every now and then. You've

seen me. Remember?" Why was I feeling defensive? Was it because I knew she had a point?

"Yes, I do. So, I'm guessing you work late, jog, sleep, and then get up and do it all over again the next morning?"

Shit. I didn't expect lunch to be an interrogation. And to think I'd fantasized about getting into her pants.

Was I that far off?

"You're right," I said, knowing that capitulation was the only way. I shook my head, all shame and sorrow.

She looked at me, head tilted as she sipped her Arnold Palmer. I was half-expecting her to pull out a note pad like a shrink.

"What's behind all that?" she asked.

If this was what she wanted to talk about, I was going to work it.

"My family didn't have much when we were kids. In fact, I was the first to go to college. As it is, I send money home to my mother. I guess you could say I have a lot of responsibility." If she was going to ask, I was going to give it to her. The raw, painful truth of who Tanner Webb was.

"Wow," she said, nodding. "I didn't know that about you."

"I know. Few people do. It's really nobody's business."

Her eyes widened. "Oh. I'm sorry. You're right. It's not my business."

I shook my head. "I didn't mean it's not *your* business. I just meant I don't tell many people. But I don't mind telling you. I don't mind at all."

Embarrassment crossed her face. Had I been too harsh?

"And what about you?" I asked. "You gonna share a secret or two with me?"

A funny look crossed her face. "Secret? I have no secrets." She shrugged.

Now that was one huge lie.

"Fair enough," I said. "So, if you're free tonight, I have an idea about something fun to do."

"Tonight? I thought this wasn't a date."

"*This* is not a date. But tonight could be." I was nothing if not persistent.

"But...well...I thought...what did you have in mind?"

Ha. Progress.

"Swing dancing."

"Swing dancing? You like swing dancing?" All levels of suspicion crossed her face.

"Actually, I've never tried it," I said. "But it sounded like fun. And I can't go alone. So you see, you'd be doing me a favor."

"Uh huh," she said. She was looking at me like I'd just told her I was Jesus.

"If I go alone, I'll look like a loser." I was all sincerity. Just a guy who wanted to swing dance. Happened every day, right?

Truthfully, I could give a shit about swing dancing. In fact, I dreaded it. But I heard chicks loved it. In fact, that they couldn't resist it.

The waiter dropped off our plates. Jayma picked up her fork and flaked off a piece of salmon.

"WELL. I guess I could go with you," she said with that sly smile that just killed me. "I do owe you and all since you got that asshole from accounting off my back."

I threw my hands in the air. "Bingo. It's really only fair."

She shrugged. "All right, then."

"Okay, awesome. And now that we've settled that, tell me about your ambitions for work."

She set her fork down, suspicion replaced by seriousness. "I studied communications in college. And I've been interested in advertising for as long as I can remember. That's why I took the job as receptionist. I've been doing it now for a couple years, but I hope I can move off the phones soon."

"Well, if you're lucky, you can join the tampon account," I said with a laugh. I was still bitter I got stuck on that campaign. Wait 'til we got a condom client someday. I'd get even with them then.

"Nah. I'm not really interested in that," she said. "I'm more into consumables. You know, food and drink. In fact, one of my friends from college works for a small organic salad dressing company."

"No kidding." Geez, she was really laying the groundwork for success. I had to love that.

"Yeah. If I can bring them into the agency, that would be huge. I think I'd definitely get a promotion then." The lady knew what she wanted.

"I'll be glad to help you in any way I can."

"Thank you. I plan to take you up on that."

"So I have to tell you something."

"Yes?" she said.

"I'd thought about asking you out for a while, even though I hardly knew you. I'm glad I finally did. Even if we are out just as *friends*." I placed air quotes around *friends*.

She looked down at her salmon. Did I piss her off or embarrass her?

"Thank you," she said, looking back up at me. "You're right. This isn't a date. But tonight, swing dancing—that could be a date. If you like."

Booyah.

That sly little smile was back on her face, the perfect contrast to those innocent-looking freckles. I had a feeling this chick had a wild side. And I was going to meet that side of her sooner rather than later.

Like tonight.

94

13

JAYMA

WELL, I HAD TO GIVE TANNER CREDIT FOR PERSISTENCE. The truth was, I wanted to go out with him just as much (I think) as he wanted to go out with me. I'd been holding out thanks to the stupid old rule, *don't shit where you eat.* But fuck it. I was a big girl, and if I wanted to see someone from work, then I would. I'd deal with the consequences later.

Plus, his nerdy glasses just about killed me.

I was a little tormented, I had to admit, about hanging out with him when I'd been with Carter just the night before. I was turning into quite the loose woman, but…to hell with it. I'd been a good girl all my life and look where that had gotten me. It was time to change things up.

And one of those changes could include becoming homeless.

Back at the office, I thanked Tanner—although I really would have liked to kiss or at least hug him—but I did need to be discreet in front of the intern at the front desk.

After work, Tanner and I grabbed an Uber across town to get to our swing dance class. I had to say, I thought it was pretty hilarious he suggested we go. I mean, who would think a hunky guy like him wanted to learn an old-fashioned dance? But hey, I was game. I'd always wanted to try swing.

We arrived at Metronome, a converted warehouse in San Francisco's Potrero Hill neighborhood. It looked like nothing from the outside, but once we were in, I realized it was set up like an old-school dance hall complete with glittery ball hanging from the ceiling.

"Hello!" a voice called from clear across the room. A little blonde woman in T-strap heels hustled over to us in a whoosh of blonde pin curls and swirling skirts.

"Hi, I'm Mel. Are you here for the swing class?" She looked so hopeful. If we hadn't been there for her class, I would have lied and said yes, anyway.

"Yes. We're told you're the master. Teach us what you will," Tanner said.

Her face lit up. "Follow me!" she said with pure glee.

She lined us up facing her and proceeded to show the class of about five couples the beginning steps of swing.

"Triple step, triple step, rock," she chanted over and

over. She said *rock* more like *rrroooock* to give us an extra beat to do some step back leaning thing. Seemed easy enough.

She turned the music on, playing this cool 1930's or 40's tune called *String of Pearls*. It had a great beat, and I was totally getting into it, dancing in place. Then she told us to grab our partners. Time for the real thing.

Only Tanner wasn't quite ready for the real thing. I'd been so focused on learning my own steps, I'd not paid attention to him, even though he was right next to me.

Mel snapped her fingers and called, "Four, three, two, *aaand* triple step…"

I took a step forward, as I was supposed to. Tanner also took a step forward, causing us to crash into each other. See, he was *supposed* to step back. My foot ended up under his, where it was promptly stomped on.

Goddamn, that hurt.

"Try again, over there," Mel called cheerfully. Everyone else in the class turned to see what was so bad that she had to holler instructions at us.

"Sorry," Tanner said. "Let's start over."

Good idea. I counted, "Four, three, two, one…"

This time, we both stepped back. *Oof.* He wasn't getting that you didn't both step forward or back at the same time. If I stepped forward, he stepped back, and vice versa.

"Wait, wait, wait," Mel cried, running over, as if

we'd broken the law of swing dancing. Of course, the other couples stopped to stare.

"When one of you steps forward, the other steps back," she said very slowly, like we were the class's remedial students.

But it didn't help. Poor Mel was defeated in a way I suspected she never had been. To cheer herself up, she turned her back on us and focused on the rest of the class, who were all doing pretty well.

"I guess I suck at this." His shoulders sagged with defeat, which tugged at my sympathies—he'd been through so much humiliation with the tampon account. I couldn't bear to see him suffer more.

I lowered my voice to a whisper. "Let's just sneak out. Mel's helping that couple over there. She won't notice 'til we're long gone."

He looked in Mel's direction. "Okay. We'll make a break for it." He grabbed my hand and we flew across the dance floor to the exit. Once we were outside, I burst out laughing. I couldn't help it.

"You know, maybe swing dancing just isn't your thing," I told him.

"Ya think?" he asked, rolling his eyes. "But I know what *is* my thing." He moved closer to me until my back was against the brick wall and his eyes were burning into mine. Holy shit.

"What is *your* thing?" I asked in a breathy voice. My heart was beginning to pound. God, I was a slut. I swallowed as he tilted my head up, and his mouth moved toward mine. The distance between us closed in an instant, and I fell, deliciously lost, into his kiss.

At first, his lips touched mine softly, the kiss growing hotter and deeper until I melted against him with everything I had. Lance had never kissed me like that. Hell, I don't think anyone ever had.

He pulled back to take his glasses off, stuffing them in a pocket. We returned to our hungry kiss before he stopped to look at me.

"You're beautiful. Just fucking beautiful."

I don't know why, but tears stung my eyes. Thank god it was dark and we were far from the street lamps. I couldn't have him thinking I was a complete nutjob, so I just looked down and murmured *thanks.*

Without a word, he waved down a cab and gave the driver his address. We held hands all the way across town, and when we arrived at his place, he turned to me.

"Would you like to spend the night?" he asked.

"I thought you'd never ask."

Slut, slut slut.

Shut up! Not now.

His apartment about blew my mind. It was in this fantastic old building on Nob Hill with views toward downtown and the beautifully lit up Bay Bridge.

"This place is insane," I said, doing a three-sixty to take in the entire vista.

He threw his jacket onto the back of a chair and walked over to a cushy velvet sofa where he sat, extending a hand to me. He might have been working freaking hard at the ad agency, but it would seem he was paid pretty well for his efforts.

I approached the edge of the sofa and stood directly in front of him. He wrapped his arms around me and stroked my ass through my skirt. He inhaled deeply, rubbing his face into my silk blouse. He was taking his time, and it was exquisite.

His hands traveled from my ass to the front of my blouse, where he opened its buttons one by one. If he hadn't started to move a bit faster, I was afraid I might explode.

He pulled my shirt open and sat back, looking at the white lace of my bra, trickling his admiring gaze over my trembling body. The way he looked at me, like I was the most beautiful woman on earth, was so fucking hot, I had to put a hand on his shoulder to steady myself. He stood up and turned me around, unzipping the back of my skirt and pushing it down my hips until it hit the floor in a puddle around my feet. I started to kick off my heels.

"No. Keep them on," he growled from behind me.

Allrighty then.

I stepped out of my skirt and kicked it aside. My blouse fell off my shoulders, and I was left standing in my bra, lace thong, and heels.

"Turn around," he said in a quiet voice.

I did as he demanded and when I faced him again, he was unbuttoning his shirt. When it dropped to the floor, I remember his amazing chest from his shirtless jog. I ran my finger over the musical notes tattooed on his neck while he fumbled with his belt and trousers. He dropped them all to the floor and we faced each other, gloriously and awesomely naked. Somewhere along the line, he'd ditched his shoes and socks. I must have missed that in my excitement.

His hand fell to his cock, a long, thick erection I couldn't move my eyes from.

"I want to fuck you, baby," he said quietly.

"Yeah? I might let you."

"I hope so. I promise you'll like it."

"Promise?" I asked.

"Oh, yeah." He reached into a small box on an end table and produced a condom, which he quickly pulled over his length.

"C'mere, beautiful," he said as he sat back on the sofa. He pushed aside the lace of my thong, and I stood before him as he buried his tongue in my pussy, where my clit hung heavy and sensitive.

"Oh my god," I murmured as he tasted me. There was a quick rush of hesitation since I'd just been with Carter, but I pushed it away. There'd be plenty of time to torment myself into a neurotic lather another day.

"You're so fucking wet. C'mon," he said, laying me back along the length of the sofa and yanking off my thong.

He balanced himself above me, one arm on either side of my head, with the swelling bulb of his cock poised right at my hungry opening.

"Are you ready for me?" he whispered. He hadn't taken his gaze from mine. It was excruciating and delicious at the same time.

"Mmmm," was all I could manage, and I nodded dreamily.

The head of his cock pushed down and just entered me where he paused. Groaning, he rocked his hips and fed me another inch or two. I was stretched so wide, the feeling so intense that I had to take deep breaths to hold off coming right away. I had no fucking idea what I was doing, but whatever it was, I was glad to be doing it.

Tanner drove his hips once more, this time burying the remaining length of his cock. We both cried out, his dick hitting me deep, and then pulling out before he drove it right back in. I banged my head back against the sofa cushions, clawing at his back, when my whole body began to shudder.

"Come for me, beautiful," he growled as he pumped my soaked pussy over and over.

"Yeah. Fuck me!" I screamed, exploding into nothing but dazed sensation. An orgasm slammed over and through me, pushing me into some abyss I didn't even know existed. Did this guy even know what he could do?

His cock pulsed inside me, and a groan turned into

a roar. He came, pumping furiously two (or was it more?) times until we both came to an exhausted stop.

His gaze burned right into mine. "Sorry about the dancing fail."

"Dancing?" I mumbled. "What dancing?"

Nothing about that evening had been a fail.

14

WYATT

"Hey there," Jayma said, opening the door to her house. If you could call it that.

"Ready? Got water and snacks?" I asked.

"Got it all right here," she said, patting her hand on a bright red backpack. She slung it over one shoulder. I stepped aside to let her lead the way from the front porch to the car. It gave me the opportunity to admire the khaki shorts that so perfectly hugged the cheeks of her cute little ass. In her hiking clothes, from her leather boots up to her fleece jacket, with the bandana tied around her braided hair, she looked like a hot little mountain mama.

Christ, my dick was already coming to life.

Get a grip, asshole.

On our way to Mount Tamalpais, my favorite hiking in all of the Bay Area, she chattered to break the ice. She left me a little tongue-tied—I mean, who wouldn't be around a woman like her?

"Have you been to Thailand?" she asked. She'd remembered my travel bug.

I nodded as we rounded a tight turn past Muir Woods. "I have."

"What did you like about it?"

"A lot of things about Thailand were really cool, but especially the food. You can go to these street markets, choose which curry you want from all these huge pots, and I swear, it costs less than a dollar. The food there was killer."

"Ugh, you're making me hungry," she said.

Hungry. I wanted her hungry. For me.

We rode in silence, my Jeep bumping along the road as we climbed to the peak of Mount Tam. Jayma had her forehead pressed to the passenger side window, watching the view unfold of San Francisco and beyond, and giving me the chance to check her out. I was dying to reach for her fingers, but it was way too soon for that. So I "accidentally" brushed my hand over the bare skin of her thigh. It was so warm and smooth, my cock sprang to attention.

She looked at me and smiled.

We pulled into the lot at the very top of Mount Tam and headed for the trail that would give us the best views. Gravel crunched under our hiking boots while we got started.

"So, how'd you get your job at the ad agency?" I asked her.

"Well, I moved to San Francisco after college and answered an ad on Craigslist for a receptionist position. I had really wanted to try for a career in advertising." She looked at me. "I'm working my way into a new position."

She had what it would take. I didn't know shit about the ad business, but I could tell.

"You'll get there. Just keep on keepin' on. I believe in persistence over quick wins," I said.

"Well, that's what I'm doing. Sticking with it." She gave me one of her mega smiles, the ones that made her freckles dance.

"I've never worked in an office. I mean, I *have* an office. But I'm only there once in a while. I like running around, taking care of customers. Keeps my mind off my dad…"

"Does it keep your mind off the travels you're missing?"

She guessed well. Or maybe it wasn't a guess. Maybe it was as obvious as the nose on my face.

I nodded slowly. "For the most part, it does. But it's always there. The thing we'd rather be doing. Happens to us all, I suppose."

"How long were you going to travel for?" We took a turn down a path lined with sky-scraping redwood trees. The canopy was so full, we were instantly immersed in what felt like dusk.

"Indefinitely. I wanted to volunteer, help install plumbing systems in poor villages, and teach the locals at the same time. Then my mom called me with news about my dad, and here I am today. I need to keep the business running to support my parents. It's the only income they have."

She stopped in front of me on the narrow trail. I was just inches from her beautiful face, and in the dim light, I could swear, her skin glowed.

"That's awesome, that you're supporting your parents," she said, reaching for my hand.

"I'm happy to do it. I know it sounds like I'm not. But there will be time for travel later. Right now, they need me." To be honest, I'd do anything for my parents.

I took her hand and brought it to my lips. Her skin smelled like lemons and fresh, clean girl.

"I wanted to ask you out the first moment I saw you," I confessed.

I brushed my lips over the back of her hand again, and then opened her palm. I moved it to my cheek and ran it up and down, reveling in her soft skin. So different from my hand, which was scratchy and callused from work. She sighed lightly and closed her eyes. It seemed like all thought exited my brain.

"Excuse me!"

Shit.

"Sorry," I said, as we stepped aside to let several hikers pass. Jesus, I thought no one else knew about this trail.

"Shall we keep going?" I asked.

Jayma took a deep breath and smiled, her nipples jutting through her shirt. I wanted to kiss each one of those sexy little babies, but I had patience when I needed it.

"Lead the way," I said, making room for her to pass. One, I wanted her to set the pace, and two, I was jonesing for any opportunity to watch her sweet ass cheeks through her little khaki shorts.

God, I sounded like an asshole.

The narrow, shaded trail opened up into a wide, gravelly one, and we were back in the full sun again. It felt so damn good I couldn't help but grab Jayma and turn her to me, where I kissed her like a starving man. Her hands flew up to my hair, where she pulled the rubber band off my ponytail. She scraped her nails over my scalp, and I fucking groaned right into her lush mouth.

This woman, who I barely knew, had this unexpected hold over me. Not in a bad way, but more like I just couldn't get her out of my mind. She was so goddamn plucky. First, she was trying her best to turn her receptionist job into something bigger. Then, she was working like hell to figure out what to do about that money pit she'd bought. And that's not even bringing up about how freaking hot she was.

But I did want to talk to her about something else. I pulled back to look at her.

"I want to help you with the house," I said.

"What? What do you mean?"

I took her hand, and we started walking again.

"I can help you. I want to help you."

She stopped and looked at me. "Thank you. That is so kind. But I don't think I can accept it. I would feel like I was taking advantage."

"I wouldn't have offered if I didn't want to. I see the potential in that house. I can't do all the work, but I can help with the kitchen and bathroom. You've already given me a twenty dollar deposit."

She laughed while her eyes got real glossy. I guess she was pretty moved that I made the offer I did. But I was glad to do it and to help someone who worked so hard. People had given me plenty of breaks. It was time I did it for someone else

She threw her arms around my neck, allowing me to bury my face in her hair. I hoped she hadn't felt my dick getting hard against her stomach, but the way she smiled at me meant she knew I was turned on. Since there was no hiding it, I pressed against her. I didn't want to be an asshole, but I had a good-sized cock and I wasn't afraid of letting her know.

"C'mon. Follow me," I said.

We left the trail and bushwhacked into the brush until we were out of sight of any other hikers. The little clearing we found gave us the perfect cover, thank god, because my raging hard-on was desperate for attention.

"You know what?" Jayma said like a naughty little flirt.

"Yeah?"

"I liked you since I first met you, too."

Bingo. I'd won the hottie lottery.

And I just about had a heart attack when she dropped her fleece jacket to the ground and sank to her knees, leaving her with perfect access to my—

Holy shit, she was going to suck my cock.

Would it have been insane of me to propose to her right there on the spot?

Get a grip, asshole.

She made quick work of the fly on my hiking shorts and pushed them to my feet. Looking up at me, she ran her fingers inside the waistband of my boxers, pulling them down with agonizing slowness. When they got low enough to release my aching cock, her head snapped back to avoid being slapped by it in the face.

"Mmmm," she murmured.

That's right, baby.

It took every ounce of my willpower not to yank her own shorts off, bend her over, and fuck her right there. But somehow, I managed to hold back and let things take their course. And follow her lead.

Which was hot as hell, I might add.

I groaned when her fingers curled around my dick, and closed my eyes when she stroked up and down my shaft. Her other hand reached for my balls, and I just about exploded in her face. Jesus, this girl.

A rustling in the bushes grabbed our attention, and I suddenly worried some park ranger was going to find us—me with my pants down, and Jayma about to suck me. I figured there would at least be a big fine for public indecency, if the ranger wanted to be a cold-hearted ass about it.

But it was just a fat old jack rabbit, stopping to take a look at us, and then disappearing as quickly as he'd joined us. I breathed a deep sigh of relief. No one was going to interrupt me and my girl, at least not then.

15

JAYMA

UGH. THERE WAS A PART OF ME THAT WHISPERED I shouldn't have been messing around with Wyatt when I'd been with Carter and Tanner just nights before. I mean, who did that? Not nice girls like me.

Guess I was done being nice.

I could make some lame excuse and walk away from them all, go back to my shitty little house, and wait for the fucking bank to come and kick me out. But I was tired of letting life just happen to me. It was *my* turn to make shit happen, and everybody better get out of my fucking way.

And when I felt Wyatt's giant dick pressing into my stomach, well, there was no way in hell I was not going to experience all he had to offer right then, and right there. If he hadn't led me into the bushes, I might have his pants down around his ankles right in the middle of the trail we'd just been on.

I gazed up at him, his dirty blond hair spilling into his eyes since I'd pulled out the ponytail holder that held his little man bun. His gorgeous tan, lined face followed my every move as my hands slid from his thighs to grip his cock.

And what a beautiful cock it was. Long, with the most perfectly shaped crown, and so thick, my fingers wouldn't even close around it. A glistening drop of precum hung from his tip, the only invitation this girl needed.

I extended my tongue to catch his salty tang, and gazed up at him again as I swallowed. His face was serious, as if he were concentrating with everything he had, but when he realized I was watching him right back, his face broke out in a beautiful grin. That just made me want to please him more.

So I took the head of his cock into my mouth and sucked until my cheeks hollowed. He groaned loudly, and for a minute, I wondered if any passersby might hear. But I realized I just really didn't give a shit. I needed to do this, to express myself physically, and to give and receive some pleasure.

I took him deeper, about as deeply as I could without gagging, and reached a hand under his balls where I gently squeezed. He groaned again, his fingers burrowing into my hair, having pushed my bandana off at some point. I wasn't sure where the damn thing went. It didn't matter. I had others.

"Goddamn..." Wyatt murmured.

I felt his balls tighten in my hand as they sent cum driving through the length of his cock and into my mouth, where it slammed the back of my throat. I swallowed all that I could, and when I couldn't take anymore, had to let the overflow run down my chin and onto the front of my shirt. It tasted like heaven.

Wyatt pulled me to my feet and held me while the life came back into my stiff legs.

"Fuck baby," was all he could say, over and over.

AFTER A GREAT DATE WITH WYATT, I returned to work with a spring in my step. His offer to help with the house gave me a new and badly needed sense of hope.

I asked the office intern to cover for me on the phones, and I slipped into a quiet conference room. I pulled some papers out of my purse.

"Hello, mortgage services," said a perky voice

My stomach was knotting.

"Um, hi. May I speak with Mr. Fraser?"

"Please hold." It seemed her perkiness was somewhat diminished when she found out I was calling for the banker who dealt with foreclosures. Yep, lady, I just called in on the loser line.

"Tony Fraser here," a dull voice said. Seemed Mr. Fraser also thought less of customers who were defaulting on their home loans.

"Mr. Fraser, it's Jayma Kersey. I'm calling about my mortgage."

Papers rustled in the background. "Oh, hello, Ms. Kersey. Let me pull up your account."

I heard lightning fast typing on a computer keyboard and several sighs. My palms were soaked, and a drip of sweat ran down my temple. I kept peering out the conference room door to make sure no one could overhear me.

"Okay, Ms. Kersey. I've got your account up right here. I can see that you're several months in default on your loan, and you have approximately two weeks before the ownership of the house reverts to the bank."

"Yes, I know that, Mr. Fraser. We discussed that last time we spoke. I'm calling you to discuss possibilities. I have some new options."

"Oh, right. Great. So what is your plan, Ms. Kersey?"

"Well. I think I can get some work done on the house and sell it pretty quickly. I just need a bit more time. But, the bank would be paid in full instead of having to take a loss by foreclosing. As for me, it would save my credit rating."

"Oh. Well," he said.

"You see, Mr. Kersey, I previously had thought I wouldn't be able to get any of the work done that the house needed, but that has changed."

"Uh-huh," he said. "Uh-huh."

Maybe he wasn't impressed with my resourceful plan?

"Will this work for the bank? I mean, isn't it better than foreclosing?" I asked.

"Ms. Kersey," he started, "I will take the proposal to my manager and see what she says."

"Really? Oh, that would be great—"

"Ms. Kersey," he interrupted, "I said I would ask. What I was going to add was that the bank is not usually amenable to arrangements that come in at the eleventh hour. But we can always ask."

"Why wouldn't the bank want to do it this way?" I asked. "That's ridiculous. You've got to work with me on this. It's a better outcome for everyone involved."

"I can see that. I'll do my best to convey your proposal."

"Well, Mr. Fraser, I really want to stress that—."

"I said I would inquire," he interrupted.

Now, I was starting to get pissed. My voice rose. There was just no stopping it.

"Look, stop being an asshole and work with me here—"

"Ms. Kersey, we don't tolerate abusive language like that. Good day," he said and hung up in my ear.

I hated banks.

SHELLE HAD FINISHED with all her dogs for the day and had agreed to meet me for a drink after work. She glided into the place looking like a million bucks. No one ever would have known that barely an hour ago, she'd been picking up dog shit in little plastic baggies.

"Hiiiiii!" she screeched, running toward me.

Oh my god. Her hair.

"What did you do to your bangs?" I asked.

Her hand flew to her head, where she started smoothing her bangs into place.

"Why? Is something wrong with them?" she asked, stiffly.

Shit. Why did I open my big mouth?

"No, not at all," I said, hoping I could backtrack.

"Well," she replied, sniffing. "I trimmed them myself. I didn't have time to go to the hairdresser. I've been way too busy with my business. "

She wouldn't look at me. Note to self—don't ever comment on Shelle's bangs again.

I waved the bartender over and ordered two beers. When he delivered them, she perked back up.

"Anyway," she said, having forgotten about my earlier insult. "What's up with your house? And all your boys?"

I took a deep breath. "Well, I might have a solution for the house. Or, at least a partial solution. And, it's tied to the guys. Well, a couple of them anyway."

"Seriously? Girl, you always land on your feet. I swear." She rolled her eyes, still fingering her bangs.

"Hardly. How is having a boyfriend dump me, sticking me with a shit show of a house, landing on my feet? You are insane."

"Okay, okay. It was just a figure of speech." She held her hands in surrender.

"So, two of the guys have offered to pitch in and help with the house. Carter, the contractor, and Wyatt, the plumber. I feel a little weird about it, though. I'm not sure."

"Are you nuts? TAKE THEIR HELP. Don't be an idiot. Swallow your pride and save your future."

"Yeah. I don't know."

"If it means you may be able to keep the house, then it's a no-brainer."

"And then there's the bank." Ugh, that familiar stomach knot came roaring back.

"Oh, yeah," she said with a sneer. I loved her for that.

"I talked to them, and of course, they're being dicks. I told them if they could get me more time, I might be able to successfully sell the house at a good price. I mean, that would be better for everyone, right?" I asked.

"Well, yeah."

"But the guy at the bank said I was bringing him my proposal at the 'eleventh hour.' I mean, what a dick. I only found out just after Lance left that he'd not been paying the mortgage. Personally, I think I'm moving pretty fast on this whole fiasco."

"Not to mention, moving fast with the dudes." She smiled at me wickedly. She'd always been a big fan of *sowing one's wild oats*. I had a lot of catching up to do, but it seemed I was well on my way. "So, do you have any other new guys I should know about?"

"I do, as a matter of fact. The odd thing is, he's best friends with my neighbor, Carter."

"What? The contractor dude?" she asked.

"Yeah. He introduced us. The guy's name is Dig, and he sells real estate. Very handsome in that dark Italian-Stallion sort of way. He called me for a date earlier today."

"But wait. How can you go out with two guys who are friends?" She looked incredulous. I couldn't blame her. I was, too.

"Right? It's definitely different. I asked him, what about Carter and wouldn't it be weird. He said not at all. So, I said yes."

Shelle pursed her lips. "It could come in handy that he's a real estate agent, too, right?"

I nodded. "Possibly."

She slapped me on my leg. "Things are so coming together for you, Jay. I knew they would."

I supposed things *looked* like they were coming together, but that was only because they couldn't get any worse.

THE RENOVATION

16

DIG

Was I glad Carter introduced me to Jayma. She was just my type, with that luscious red hair, adorable freckles, and tight little body. And she was clearly sharp as a whip, too. I was so over good-looking girls with nothing upstairs.

It wasn't surprising Carter hooked me up with her. He knew my type, probably better than I did. We'd shared girls a few times over the years and it worked out great.

Thank god, we had none of those ridiculous jealousy issues that do nothing but fuck you up. No cock-blocking games like we saw so many other dudes get into. Maybe it was because we were thick as brothers, having stuck together since Carter's family had pretty much taken me in. And if anything, we were even closer as adults, referring business to each other, loving the same ladies. You name it.

I'd been thinking about Jayma since we'd sat down for drinks with her. When I'd checked with Carter to see if I could ask her out, he was pleased to say yes. He'd known I'd like her. He told me the guy she'd been living with had made off with another woman. What a fucking idiot.

It was no easy task getting the evening off. Real estate was pretty much a 24/7 job. You had to accommodate your clients' schedules. If someone could only see a property in the middle of the night, as long as no one was living there, I'd take them to see it. I did everything I could to take care of my clients. They, in turn, took care of me by sending everyone they knew to me.

I had a coworker cover for me, and I'd scheduled so many clients for the following day that I was going to be running from dawn to dusk. But it was worth it to have some time to get to know Jayma. The clients would still be there in the morning.

I had a low-key but classic San Francisco evening planned. We were going to meet in North Beach, the city's old Italian neighborhood, on the corner of Grant and Union streets, and go from there. I was busting ass to get there early, though, so she wouldn't have to wait on a street corner for me. Carter's dad, who'd been more of a father to me than my own, always told us to never keep a lady waiting. When I arrived, I had to wipe my forehead down with a handkerchief— another thing Carter's dad always insisted on. He'd said hankies might have been old-fashioned, but having one could get you out of multiple jams. Like just then.

And hell if I wasn't doubly glad I had one when I saw Jayma bouncing toward me down the street wearing a big, gorgeous smile, and a slim dress showing off her trim figure. For some inexplicable reason, I broke out in *another* sweat, even though I was standing there doing nothing.

What was it about this woman? God help me.

"Hi!" she said in a big, bright voice, throwing her arms around me for a hug. She smelled freaking awesome. I didn't want to let go.

Cool it, asshole.

"Hey, gorgeous. Great to see you again," I said.

"I just love this part of the city," she said, looking around. "It's so charming. Kind of like going back in time. Although, I don't know how many Italians live here anymore." She laughed.

"No kidding. But at least the place is still full of killer places to eat. The Italians might have moved out of the neighborhood, but they left their restaurants behind."

Seriously, I was grateful for that. I lived for Italian food.

"Speaking of food, I'm starving," she said.

"Good, 'cause so am I. Have you been to Tony's?"

"You mean the world-famous pizza joint? I've never been, and I've always wanted to give it a try."

We strolled a couple blocks toward Tony's, and

when we arrived, I placed my hand on the small of her back and guided her in the door. Tony's was a typical old Italian joint with exposed brick, shelves of Chianti bottles lining the walls, and big paintings of the Roman Coliseum and other Italian landmarks. There was even a fountain in the corner with a little Leaning Tower of Pisa in the middle—tacky and hilarious, but charming in a way that only Italian restaurants could be.

We ordered a couple different kinds of pizza and a bottle of wine and got to talking.

"So, you have some work to do on your house, huh?" I asked.

She sighed. "Yeah, do I. But I think I might be getting some help with it. There's still hope."

"Right. Flipping houses is a hard business. You have to have enough money, and then your contractors, all lined up at the right time. If you don't turn it around fast enough, you could face a massive loss." I'd seen it before, having helped people both buy and sell fixer-uppers. It was a tough game.

"All *was* going according to plan," she said sadly. "Then the boyfriend bailed."

"Jesus, that sucks. But it sounds like you've found some people who can help." I caught her gaze. "Like me."

A pink blush lit up her face. "Gosh, Dig. Thank you. I really appreciate that. Are you sure it's okay?"

I reached across the table and took her hand. No use in pussyfooting around.

"I offered. I would not help if I didn't think I sincerely could."

"Well, thank you. It's very generous," she said, gripping my fingers back.

"I've helped folks with houses like this before. There are plenty of people out there looking for a turnkey house to get into, one where they don't have to do anything. I can find buyers for you once the place is all fixed up."

I could swear her eyes were looking extra-shiny all of a sudden. Was she going to cry?

She cleared her throat and let go of my hand, grabbing her napkin to dab her eyes.

"I'm sorry. I get emotional about this stuff. It's been a real rollercoaster."

"You won't lose the house. Not if I have anything to do with it. And I know Carter feels the same way."

She took a deep breath and a smile returned to her face.

"What's up with you guys, anyway? Both wanting to date the same woman?"

I'd been waiting for this part of the conversation. It was inevitable.

And she deserved answers. After all, Carter's and my tastes were more than a little unconventional.

"Carter and I have been in relationships with the same woman before. It's not like we set out looking for an arrangement like that. It just sort of evolved."

"Really?" she asked, diving into her first slice of pizza. Man, did I love a woman who could eat.

"Carter and I, we have amazingly similar tastes. Maybe I should say identical tastes. It started a long time ago, when we fell for the same woman. She suggested we both date her, so we did. It was fantastic. When one of us was busy, the other could be with her. And sometimes all three of us would go out."

She put down her fork, looking uncomfortable. "Um, well, do you guys…you know?"

"What? Oh, do Carter and I get it on?" I had to laugh. That question always came up. "No, that's not our thing. Not that there's anything wrong with it," I added with a wink.

"Oh. I was just wondering," she said, going back to her pizza.

I smiled quietly, drinking her in.

"Jayma, I gotta tell you, I've wanted to take you out since the first time I met you."

There was that blush again. Shit, I was in trouble.

"Thank you. That's really sweet. I'm so flattered. And I'm interested in you, too. But Carter had already asked me out, and since you were his friend, I figured it wasn't kosher."

"Oh, it's kosher," I said, unable to tear my gaze from those eyes.

"Okay. Wow," she said with raised eyebrows.

Thank god, the white tablecloth covered my lap. It did an excellent job of hiding my growing erection.

"Jayma?"

"Yes?"

"Have you ever been *shared*?" I asked her.

"Um, no, no I have not."

Shit, she looked scared.

But that was okay, because I was ready to teach her there was nothing to be scared of.

17

JAYMA

JAYMA

Good lord. *Shared?*

Dig sat across the table from me with his gorgeous black hair, dark eyes, and perfectly chiseled jaw, and he not only wanted me, but it was okay with him that his friend Carter did, too.

What. The. Fuck.

First, I wasn't sure I got the whole sharing thing. Nobody did that. Did they?

But I'd work all that shit out later. Tonight was my night with Dig, and damn if the food at the world famous Tony's wasn't completely amazing. Pizza with a delicate thin, crunchy crust.

I was in heaven. And it didn't hurt that we were on our second bottle of red.

Slow down, girl.

But seriously, how often does one sit across from a freaking god of a man, consuming mind-blowing pizza and wine, and have him offer not only his real estate services, but also himself and his best friend?

Was Shelle right? Maybe things *were* beginning to go my way.

"Well. This is...kind of amazing," I told him. I couldn't find words to explain how weird his proposal was, and yet how much it turned me on.

He nodded as he handed the waiter his credit card.

"If it's too much, I understand. We understand. It has to work for all parties involved." Good grief, it sounded like a business transaction. And then he flashed me his stunning smile. Damn him, he'd made me all gooey inside. I'd thought men like him only existed in the movies. Little did I know they were walking the streets of San Francisco, brokering real estate deals. And eating pizza.

"What happened with your family?" I asked. It was really none of my damn business, but I'd told him my dirt, and if he was comfortable talking about *sharing* a woman with his best friend, well, anything and everything was on the table.

"You mean why did Carter's family basically take me in?" he asked.

"Yes. If you don't mind my asking," I added, to be polite.

"Well, it's kind of simple, really. My mother bailed, and my dad didn't deal with it so well."

The sadness that settled over his face made my heart break.

"I'm sorry to hear that."

His gaze held mine. "Thank you. It was a shitty thing to go through, but on the other hand, such a miracle that Carter's parents stepped up to the plate." He shook his head as if after all these years, he still couldn't believe his good fortune.

"That was so generous of them."

"You're not kidding. I owe them everything. Carter stuck by me, just like his parents did. It was his mom who got me into real estate."

I reached for his hand across the table, and when I did, I could swear something shot right up my arm and straight down to my core. I loved how he didn't take for granted the great family he found.

We walked out of the restaurant to our waiting Uber.

"Your place?" he asked.

To be honest, no discussion was necessary. We knew what we had to do.

He climbed into the car after me, sliding close, bringing my hand to his lips. His gaze locked with mine as he gave me light kiss after light kiss.

Of course, I wanted to go to my fucking house. Or his house. Or anyone's house. Whichever was closer. How about behind that dumpster over there, in that alley?

"Yeah," I said softly. I guess that was all the invitation he needed, because in two seconds, he was devouring my lips like he was dying of thirst. The Uber driver could have kidnapped us, that's how oblivious we were to everything around us.

When we pulled up to my house, we had to part—you can't very well climb out of a car when you're sucking face.

And don't you know, my next-door neighbor and booty call from just a few nights before was just pulling up to his house.

That's right. Carter Bannon.

Busted. Goddammit.

"Yo, Jayma, Dig. How're you guys?" he called, grabbing groceries from the back of his truck.

I looked around for a rock to crawl under.

"Hey, Car. We're good, man. Just ate at Tony's in North Beach," Dig answered.

"Oh, nice. I love that place," Carter said with a big smile, heading into his house. "You guys have a good night."

Dig took my hand and looked at me. Just another day at the office for those guys, apparently.

They were completely unfazed at having run into each other with me in tow.

I, on the other hand, wanted to curl up and die. I fumbled with my key, trying to get inside the house as fast as possible. I pulled Dig in and slammed the door.

"Are you okay?" he asked when I breathed in relief.

Was he really asking me that?

I looked up at him. "Wasn't it a little weird, running into Carter like that? I feel kind of like I was busted."

Confusion crossed his gorgeous face. "No. Not at all."

He reached for my hair and ran his fingers through it. "But I can see you're concerned. You don't need to be."

"If you say so." If he wasn't going to trip out, then neither was I. I leaned into him, parting my lips to kiss him.

I was going to relax and enjoy the ride.

He pulled back and looked around the living room. "So this is the place, huh?"

Every person who walked through my front door was amazed the first time they saw the house. Actually, some were still amazed the second and third time they saw its shitty condition. Dig was no different.

I followed his gaze. "Yup. This would be it." I waved my arm for the big reveal.

He turned back to me and said with absolute sincerity, "It has great potential. It really does. Why don't you show me the rest?"

Why don't I just show you the bedroom, where I can tear your clothes off and rub all up against—

Jesus. What was I becoming? A nympho?

Eh, there'd be time to worry about that later.

I brought Dig to my bedroom, the only place in the house not in a complete shambles. Before Lance had bailed, we'd had the room gutted, hung new drywall and trim, and replaced the windows. A nice paint job and a polished floor later, and it looked like something out of a magazine. 'Course, it was filled with my nice furniture.

Too bad about the rest of the house.

As I looked around the room, my mind wandering to what I was going to do about said house, Dig came up behind me. The moment he put his hands on my shoulders, my stress about the place dissolved into a silly little concern that was a waste of time. There were better things at hand, literally and figuratively.

I arched my neck, letting my head fall into onto his rocky chest. His fingers traveled over my shoulders and down the front of my body, where they stopped at my nipples. Through the fabric of my thin dress, he took hold of them and pulled until I cried out.

Good lord that hurt. But something about it also felt good. And alive—so very alive.

As he rolled my nipples through his fingers, he bent to kiss the side of my neck. I tilted my head to give him better access and don't you know, his little nips and nibbles were so intoxicating I could barely continue to stand. Without letting go of me, he walked me toward the bed, where he lay me across the comforter onto my stomach.

First, he removed my shoes, and then he undid the long zipper on the back of my dress. With a little wriggling, he worked it up my body and over my head to where it landed on the floor with a little whoosh. That left me in my thong panty and bra. Being facedown, I couldn't see what he was doing behind me, but I could hear his breath rasping at my undressed state.

The bed shifted with his weight. He'd climbed up and straddled me, one knee on either side of my hips. I was pinned in place.

His hot breath was on my ass in an instant, followed by his lips. They brushed back and forth over my cheeks, getting closer and closer to the thin strip of lace running up my crack. He pressed his tongue into the groove, about driving me wild with sensation. I arched my back to push my bum up to his face, and he let out a soft groan.

"Fuck, baby," he murmured. "This ass is the stuff of dreams. I can't get enough…"

He began to slide my thong down my hips, where it rested around the tops of my thighs. This gave him full access to my backside, leaving me in an explosive state. I wanted him to do something—anything—to grant me a little release.

But what I didn't expect was to feel his tongue on my ass. Was this the new thing? Was everybody doing this and I was only just finding out about it?

His tongue on my most private part was pure heaven. He jumped off me, and in a swift motion, had pulled my thong down and off my legs. He pushed my knees apart just enough to fit his own between them. I could feel his hot gaze on my openness. He pushed and kneaded my ass cheeks, exposing me even further. His breath was on me again, followed by a tongue that stroked down to my pussy. I was so wet, I dripped onto the bed beneath us.

"You good, baby? You doin' okay?" he asked.

"Mmmmm," was all I could say.

His hand fell to my pussy, tickling the insides of my soaked lips. They found my opening and teased me there, a finger popping in and out, up to the knuckle. Then in an instant, he filled me with two fingers and began pistoning with a fury revealing a passion that scared—and thrilled me—at the same time.

I knew he was going to pull a shattering orgasm out of me as I started to shriek for breath and pound my hands on the bed. I arched my hips back and against his thrusts to increase the sensation, my body quaking beyond anything I could control.

"God, yeah. Oh, give it to me," I begged.

"Do you have a condom?" he asked.

"Yeah. Yes, nightstand," was all I could mutter.

I heard the snap of the condom on his cock, and his strong arms pulled me up to my knees. He bent over me, pushing my head down on the bed, and positioned his erection against my opening.

I wanted it so fucking bad, I couldn't see.

"Please…" I begged. I needed it; I needed him. I needed to forget the mess my life was, and for a moment, believe my beautiful bedroom was all there was in the world—with Dig in it, of course.

"Are you ready, baby?" he growled.

"Yes. Yes, please. Fuck me, Dig," I whispered.

He eased into me with a groan. I spasmed instantly, approaching another climax that threw my freaking brain offline. A swirling sensation took over, leaving my every nerve screaming.

A guttural moan from behind pushed me over my edge. I bucked against Dig's cock, convulsing as he met my thrusts. He pumped me one more time before we slammed to a stop and collapsed on the bed, his arms holding me tightly.

"God, baby. You are hot," he said, twirling a strand of my hair around his finger. I watched him pull it tighter and tighter and then let it snap back to a curl.

I flipped over to face him, our gazes locked.

"Damnnnn," I said, running a finger over his perfect chest. "That was amazing."

"That," he said, "was us just getting started."

"OH MY GOD, SHELLE," I panted the minute after Dig left.

"Why are you calling me so late?" she groaned. It was kind of shitty of me to bother her at eleven p.m., seeing how early she got up for her doggy duty. But this was an urgent matter.

"Shelle, hear me out. I need to talk. These are desperate times."

In the background, I heard her taking a sip of the water that she always kept by her bed. She cleared her throat.

"Okay. Okay, I'm here. What the hell happened? Did the roof blow off the house?"

"Don't make fun of my house when I'm in a crisis," I barked.

Long sigh. "Okay, geez. Sorry. For chrissakes, would you spill it?"

"I just went out with the real estate guy, Dig."

"Okay. Well, I take it that since you're calling me so late that means you fucked him? Hey, how come he didn't stay over?"

Why did she have to ask these kinds of questions?

"He had to get up early. Anyway, yes, we had sex. Massive, hot, nasty sex. He was amazing."

She yawned. "Okay. I'm happy for you. Now why are you calling me so fucking late?"

"Because...he's the fourth guy I've dated in the last week and a half. I think I'm an official slut."

"Oh god. I don't know if you're an official slut, but you are an official idiot. What are you so freaked about?"

"Let me spell it out for you, Shelle. I like them all. I don't know what to do," I whined.

"You seem to be doing okay to me."

"I can't date four guys. I have to choose one."

"Okay. Then choose one," she said. I heard her sinking back into her bed. I was losing her.

"How can I? Carter, my hot neighbor, is so sweet. He wants to fix up my crappy house. Tanner, from work, is built like a god and is helping me get ahead in advertising. Wyatt, my world-traveling plumber, has offered to put some time in on the house, too. And the last guy, Dig, the tall, dark, and handsome one, wants to sell the house when it's done."

"Oh. My. Wow." I had her attention now.

"And they all seem to like me, just like I like them."

"Okay," Shelle said. "This is what you have to do."

"Yeah?" I asked.

"You need to be honest with them. All of them. Tell them how you feel, and that it's tormenting you. I'll bet they'll all date you until you can clearly choose one. And if any of them bail, then you'll know he wasn't for you."

"Oh my god. I don't know if I can."

"I don't see any choice. You can be honest with them all and maybe you'll end up with someone, and maybe not. But if you're not honest, you'll definitely end up with no one."

18

CARTER

I WASN'T SURE WHETHER JAYMA WOULD GO FOR IT OR not, but she finally agreed to accept my help. Not that she had much choice. I mean, she was down to the wire. The bank was ready to snap up the house with their greedy little hands, leaving her god knows where. Shit, if I really thought about it, I was just as excited about helping her as I was in giving the bank the big old middle finger.

If we could pull it off.

We had to fix up the place and sell it. And we had two weeks.

The good news was that Dig's date with her had been awesome, just as mine had. We didn't know if she'd accept the offer of dating us both, but we were patient.

And—she was coming to stay with me.

Yup. While her house was worked on, she couldn't

very well stay there—the electric and plumbing had to be cut off. So I offered her and her cat an extra room—my house was huge, anyway. No strings attached, of course. But if she did want to share my bed with me from time to time, well, I'd be quite happy about that.

I ran across the lawn to her house and rang the doorbell. The one that was hanging out of its socket by a wire.

Ugh. What was I getting myself into?

The door flew open, and there stood my redheaded beauty.

Well, she wasn't mine, per se. But a guy could always hope.

"You all packed up?" I asked. God, she looked cute in her jeans and sneakers.

She took a deep breath and looked around the house. "I think so. I just have these couple bags here."

I picked them up while she locked the door behind her. Although I couldn't imagine anyone trying to break into the place.

"Are you sure it's okay for me to stay?" she asked, as we walked over the lawn to my place.

I pushed open my front door and let her enter first.

"It's fine, seriously. I wouldn't have offered if it wasn't. I've got tons of room. More than I can use. And I can't wait to get going on your house. I mean, it's a contractor's dream to be able to take something down to the studs and build anew."

I dropped her bags in the living room.

She shook her head. "I can't tell you how grateful I am for this. But really, I don't see how we can pull this off as fast as we need to. And you're crazy to front me the money."

I walked over to her and tucked a strand of hair behind her ear

"I have my calendar cleared and my best guys coming tomorrow. You won't believe how fast we work. My crew kicks ass. That house is gonna sell, and we'll all make our money back."

"Well, then." She gave me a naughty little smile. "I'd love to show you how grateful I am."

Now that's what I'm talking about. Shit, yeah.

In about two seconds flat, she had me pushed up against the kitchen counter, her lips pressed to mine while she fumbled with my belt and fly.

And my cock, which was already twitching, jumped to full attention.

She pulled me out of a tangle of boxer shorts and blue jeans and stroked my hard length. Her grip was beyond perfection as she rounded the head of my cock and ran her fingers back down to its root.

Fuck yeah. I think my eyes rolled back in my head. I gripped the counter as if my life depended on it. I didn't care *what* she did to me at that point. It was all good.

But when her tongue lapped at the precum dripping from my head, my gaze snapped to attention. I wasn't going to miss this beauty going to town on my hard-on.

Her lips encircled me, taking an inch at a time until I figured I was partway down her throat. I'd never seen anything like it. She gazed up at me with those freaking gorgeous eyes. They fluttered closed, and she lapped me up and down until her cheeks hollowed from the suction. I had to focus on the wall clock on the other side of the room to keep from blowing my wad right then and there in her pretty mouth.

And she wasn't making it easy on me. She no sooner released my cock from her mouth when she moved it aside and stretched her tongue to my balls.

Jesus Christ.

She devoured as much of my sac as she could, and I had to admit, I couldn't hold back any longer.

"Shit, baby, I'm gonna come. I'm gonna come."

She maneuvered my cock back to her mouth, and with an extended tongue, let me shoot right into her open mouth like it was some kind of goddamn recepta-cle. She smiled as she looked at me, swallowing an entire mouthful of cum, licking her lips like it was the best thing she'd ever tasted.

I gripped her arms and pulled her back to standing.

"Holy shit, baby," I said.

"Hey, guys," a voice said from the kitchen doorway.

Poor Jayma shrieked and moved to cover my naked dick, as if I gave a shit that anyone might see me with a partial hard-on, especially Dig.

"Dude!" I said, tucking myself back in my pants.

Jayma looked from one of us to the other, eyes frantic.

And Dig and I just smiled.

"Hey, gorgeous," he said, walking to her and planting a big one on her mouth. After a moment, she fell into his arms, which was fucking hot to see, especially when she'd just sucked me to within an inch of my life.

I pulled some beers out of the fridge, cracked one open for myself, and settled down into one of my kitchen chairs to watch Jayma with Dig. Damn, that guy moved fast. Her top was already off, and as he moved in on her bottoms, she grabbed her own tits and began pulling and twisting their nipples.

If I hadn't just come, I'd be stroking myself to beat the band. Those two looked great together, Jayma with her fair skin and fiery hair, and Dig, the perfect dark contrast. He looked over at me just quick enough to let me know he was ready to really turn up the heat. Reaching down, he hoisted Jayma up 'til her legs wrapped around his back. He brought her over to me and sat her in my lap. Her cute little butt rubbed against my dick, which by then, was getting hard again.

Goddamn, the effect the woman had on me.

Dig positioned her so she sat on me with her back to my chest. I put my hands on her waist to hold her in place, and she let her head drop back onto my pecs. Dig parted her legs and draped them outside of mine, leaving her about as wide open as she could get. It was as if she were laid out for sacrifice on the altar of my lap.

Ha, I'd have to share that thought with Dig, later.

Speaking of Dig, he stepped back to admire his handiwork. His face was dark with hunger, his gaze running over her as if he didn't know where to stop. If I didn't know him better, shit, I'd probably be afraid of him. He dropped to his knees, and settling back on his haunches, ran his hands up Jayma's legs. When he closed in on her inner thighs, she arched back against me, squirming and moaning.

Shit, this girl was everything. Beautiful, sexy, smart, and a go-getter. She wasn't waiting around for some guy to take care of her like so many other women I'd known. She wanted to make her own way, and I loved that about her.

Dig dove into her wide-open pussy like I knew he would, running up and down her slit, spreading her lips wide open with his swirling tongue. Jayma, shuddering and convulsing, gripped my arms until her fingers left marks.

"Oh, god," she cried.

Dig zeroed in on her clit and began to suck. I couldn't see much from where I sat, but he must also have filled her with a finger or two and started pumping because she was bucking against me like she was being drilled.

A spark flew through me, one that told me being

where I was at that moment in time was perfect, that I was in exactly the right place, doing exactly what I should be. Jayma trembled, sandwiched between us. A cry broke from her pretty lips as an orgasm at Dig's hand—and tongue—drove her right over her edge. When she came, screaming and clawing at both Dig and me, I didn't think I could take much more. But I'd had my turn, and now, it was his.

He jumped to his feet and positioned himself right in front of Jayma's face, ripping off his shirt, and letting his pants fall to the floor. His hand flew to his cock, which he presented to her so she could taste his precum. She moaned as she consumed his tang, then let go of my arms and pulled him into her mouth with a grip on his balls. Fuck, it was like she was starving.

No complaints here.

19

JAYMA

O HMYGOD, OHMYGOD. I WAS WITH TWO GUYS AT THE same time, something I'd fantasized about since, well, I was old enough to fantasize. It was naughty and dirty, and every bit as freaking amazing as you might think.

God, Dig was attractive, with his dark, powerful heat that seemed to suck all the air out of the room. Shit, Carter was gorgeous too, but Dig was the one I was looking at, at that very moment. And just when I thought I couldn't take anymore, sitting there, spread-eagled on Carter's lap, Dig started to finger bang me while licking my clit.

"Are you a dirty girl, Jayma?" Carter murmured in my ear.

But I couldn't answer. I was beyond capable of speech. I lay my head back against his strong chest and let a long and drawn-out orgasm roll over me. Dig stood and offered me his cock, which I hungrily took into my mouth.

I'd sucked two cocks in one night.

And I was loving it.

I took Dig as deeply as I could until he banged the back of my throat. With one hand under his balls, I bobbed my head up and down on him until he groaned.

"Look at our girl, Carter, taking me so deep," Dig growled, rocking his hips into my mouth.

"She's sweet, isn't she?" Carter replied.

Wait. Did he said say *our girl*?

When did that happen?

"Fuck, your mouth feels good. Can I fill you with my cum, baby?" Dig asked.

"Mmmm." I pulled away, licking his crown. "Yes, please."

Holding my head, he drove his cock back into my mouth before pulling it out again. Back and forth he went until he roared. Hot cum pumped down my throat until I could hardly breathe. I looked up to find his gaze locked on my face with the most beautiful, happy, and peaceful smile, with me situated on Carter's lap, where he held me close and tight.

Why had I waited so long to do a threesome?

Dig pulled me to my feet and Carter left the room, returning with a plushy pink bathrobe that fit me perfectly.

"You got this for me?" I asked, looking at him.

"No, *I* did not." He looked at Dig. "*We* did."

Tears burned at my eyes, but I didn't let them fall. I didn't want to ruin the moment with my excess-sentimentality.

But I have to say, Lance had never done anything like that for me.

Not bought me a spontaneous gift, nor given me an orgasm like that. Fuck that loser.

We staggered over to the living room sofa, where I lay with my head in Dig's lap and my feet in Carter's.

"So, dude, how long can you stay?" Carter asked Dig.

Did he need to be somewhere?

Dig shrugged. "As long as I want. My bag is in the car." He and Carter reached over me to clink beer bottles.

"Um, what do you mean you have a bag in the car?" I asked, craning my neck to look at each of them.

"Well, darlin'," Carter started. "We thought we'd let you test drive us."

"Huh?" I mumbled.

Dig stepped in. "Jayma, as you know, we like to share. And we'd like to share *you*."

"And we thought the best way to introduce you to our little lifestyle was to all live under one roof. See how it goes," Carter said.

"In fact," Dig continued, "we also invited the other two guys you are seeing."

"*What?*" I jumped off the sofa and looked at both of them, my heart pounding. Slamming against my chest in fact. This wasn't funny. Not at all. I pulled the tie on my bathrobe tighter.

"Your girlfriend Sharon—"

"—Shelle, her name is Shelle, Dig," Carter interrupted.

"Right, sorry," Dig said. "Your friend Shelle contacted all of us and suggested we have a meeting, given your predicament. We took it one step further and invited the other guys to move in to make it easier for you to make your choice."

"No, no, no, no. Who *does* that? It's creepy and weird," I said.

What. The. Fuck.

First off, Shelle was officially no longer my best friend. It was over between us. But first, I would kill her. Or at least yell at her really bad.

Next, how had she tracked the guys down anyway?

Actually, from what I'd shared with her, it was probably really easy. I was still going to kill her.

Carter looked at Dig.

"Dude. She thinks we're creepy and weird," he said, shaking his head.

Dig's brow furrowed. Was that hurt on his face?

"Gee. I think we misread you, Jayma. I'm really sorry."

"Wait. What? Okay, hold on, everyone." I needed to think. Except that I couldn't. Thanks to our sexy little threesome, my poor head was muddled. My thoughts were mush.

These guys were great. They were freaking gorgeous, successful, nice as hell, and they wanted to help me out of my shitty predicament.

They outshone Lance in every category.

Which I suppose wasn't really that hard.

Lance was gradually becoming a distant memory, while my new "friends" made me see that I deserved better. They wanted to treat me like a queen. And they wanted me to believe I *deserved* to be treated like one, too.

How did I get so damn lucky?

Or was this a short-lived fluke?

"Um, *the other guys?*"

Dig looked at Carter, then me. "We understand there are two other guys you've recently dated, named, um—" He looked back at Carter, who answered for him.

"Tanner and Wyatt. The guys' names are Tanner and Wyatt," Carter said.

"Right. Thanks. Anyway, Tanner and Wyatt will be joining us here. They'll be helping to reno the house, and at the same time, you can get to know us all better."

"And…the idea is I'll choose at the end?"

They both nodded. "If you want."

"Yeah."

"Mmm hmmm."

Did I already say holy shit?

Because—holy shit.

"Hey, Jayma," Shelled chirped into the phone.

In about thirty seconds, she was not going to be sounding quite as cheerful.

I took a deep breath. But it didn't help. I exploded.

"What the fuck, Shelle? Telling the guys about each other and then sharing their information? Are you out of your mind?" I was trying to keep my voice down so Carter and Dig couldn't hear me downstairs. It wasn't working.

"God, you don't have to yell," she said testily. "I was doing you a favor. You were wallowing in your own pity party. This will force you to make some decisions and get on with your life."

She did *not* just say that.

I took a deep breath. "You have got to be kidding. I was doing just fine until you arranged for me to live with *four* guys—*four guys!*"

She giggled. "I know, right? Doesn't it sound awesome? Hey, can I have a chance at your leftovers?"

She did have a point. It might very well be awesome. Weird, but awesome.

However, I wasn't done being mad.

"It's not funny. Stop laughing," I told her.

But she didn't stop laughing. She couldn't. And her laughter always got me.

Okay, it *was* kind of funny. Me, living with four guys at once, who were going to work on my house.

Sounded like a damn game show. Or a reality show.

One where I might win.

"C'mon, Jay. Lighten up. It will be fine. Think of all the great sex you're gonna have. In fact, do you think I could come over some time?"

"No, you may not come over. I don't trust you to behave."

"Aww, seriously? That's kind of crappy and ungrateful."

"Really?" I asked. "In what universe is it okay for you to gather the guys I'm dating and get them all to move into a house together? Where I also happen to be living?"

"You know, Jay," she said with irritation, "some day, you'll thank me for this. You'll see how I've helped you—"

"I gotta go, Shelle. I'll talk to you later." I hung up on her mid-sentence. It was a bitchy thing to do, but I'd apologize later.

I sat down on the edge of the bed in the room that was to be mine until—well, I didn't know until when. I mean, if we managed to renovate and sell the house before the bank could make off with it, I'd have to find a new place to live, and if the bank took the house, I'd need a new place to live anyway. Who knew how long I'd be at Carter's? With Dig. And Tanner. And Wyatt.

And how in god's name would I choose? I liked

them all, truly. There was just something about each one—wonderful in his own way. But still different.

I flopped back onto my bed. Shit, I was exhausted. The drama was taking it out of me.

And, I had a big day at work coming up. I was meeting with Mr. Renner to talk about my "future" at the agency. I'd taken the bull by the horns and set it up myself. I figured if I didn't make it happen, it surely never would.

TANNER

Well. Now I'd heard it all.

Jayma's next door neighbor, a total stranger to me, invited me to move in with him. And two other guys. For a total of four dudes under one roof.

Oh, and did I mention Jayma would be living there? And her cat?

Um…what?

At first, I thought the dude was crazy. Certifiably insane. And maybe he was. But the more I thought about it, and my desire to break out of my corporate rut where I had to think about tampons, and hear the particulars of my female colleagues' monthly cycles, the more I thought it wasn't any crazier than the life I was already living.

So I said yes. What was the worst that could happen?

I might not end up with Jayma, but hey, I could

walk away with some cool new guy friends. And Carter told me I could help with the house reno—he'd teach me whatever I wanted to learn.

It was going to be great to roll up my sleeves and do some hard, physical work for a change. And not hear a goddamn word about tampons.

I drove over to Jayma's neighborhood and parked at Carter's just next door. And what a contrast it was. His, in pristine condition, a huge, sleek, mid-century modern home that had clearly been updated by someone with great taste and a lot of talent. Hers— well, it had potential.

The door flew open when I rang the bell, and Jayma stood there in a sexy little dress and high heels. Guess she'd gotten used to the idea of shacking up with a bunch of dudes.

"Tanner! Come in, come in. Oh, I'm so glad you're here," she said, throwing her arms around my neck. I loved the way she smelled, so fresh with the slightest hint of some spicy perfume.

"Hey, baby," I said, looking around. "What an amazing place."

"I know, right? Isn't it great? It's modern, but not too modern."

"I know what you mean. Hey, how did your meeting with Mr. Renner go today?"

She pursed her lips. What was that all about?

"Oh, I'll tell ya later. First, I want to show you around."

I'd been in only one other mid-century modern house before, and it had been in pretty sorry shape. But this one was perfection, with exposed beams across the ceiling, a gigantic stone fireplace, and super sleek furniture. Who the hell was this guy, Carter?

"Great place," I said.

"Isn't it? Want to see your bedroom?"

I followed her up an open staircase—admittedly with one eye on her ass the entire time—to a killer room with a comfy-looking bed and flat-screen TV on the wall. Jackpot. I'd be nice and comfortable there.

"You like it?" she asked with a hopeful expression.

"No complaints. None at all." I dropped my bag on the floor and pulled her to me.

It took every ounce of strength I had to not pull up her dress, yank down her panties, and bury my face between her soft thighs until she creamed all over me.

Somehow managed to hold back, but I knew my resolve would not last long. We either had to get out of my room or get down to business.

I preferred business, but we had other things to take care of, first. Like meeting the other guys, my new housemates. I peeled my hands off her taut little body and brought her fingers to my lips for a kiss.

"You gonna introduce me to the others?" I asked.

"Sure thing. You ready?"

"I'm always ready, baby." I gave her one of my cheesy winks, and she laughed. I loved that sound. I rustled through my bag to grab something and followed her back down the stairs to a wide-open kitchen where two guys stood drinking Stellas.

I strode in, extending my hand.

"I'm Tanner. Good to meet you. I brought a little something to celebrate." I produced a bottle of Johnny Walker Blue.

"Whoa, dude. That is seriously generous. I'm Carter, and this is Dig."

"Welcome aboard, my friend," Dig said.

"Great place you have here, Carter."

"I'm very glad to be sharing it with you," Carter answered. "All of you. We're just missing Wyatt."

"Hello. I'm still here," Jayma said from behind me.

That got a laugh out of everyone.

"Sorry, darlin'," I said, draping an arm around her shoulder.

"What are we celebrating?" she asked, nodding at the expensive scotch.

I shrugged. "Nothing and everything."

"I'll drink to that," Carter said, pouring each of us a couple fingers.

"Cheers," I said, "to new friends and adventures." Glasses clinked all around.

"So Tanner, you work in advertising?" Dig asked.

God that scotch was good. "I do. I'm a desk job kind of guy. Unlike our builder, here." I pointed at Carter.

"Well, that makes two of us," Dig said. "I'm in real estate."

"Oh, nice. What a great field to be in here in San Francisco," I said.

"Well, it's damn competitive, but it's lucrative, too. Feels like I work around the clock," Dig replied.

"Speaking of working around the clock," I said, "Carter, what's the plan for Jayma's house?"

She smiled. "Yeah, Carter, what *is* the plan for my house?"

He nodded. I admired a man who was ready. "Got my crew coming at seven a.m. We'll be able to dive right in since Jayma already has the permits from the city. We'll gut the rooms that need it, haul away the waste, and start putting up new drywall."

"Sounds like a plan. I'd love to pitch in where I can. I want to learn some home improvement skills. Just put me to work," I said.

"Maybe he'll be your bitch, Carter," Jayma said with a naughty laugh.

"Hey now, don't give the guy any ideas," I said.

"So do you think you can get the work done fast?" Dig asked. "I can start lining up some buyers."

"I'm not sure. I do feel hopeful, though. We're cutting it close. But we're going to try our damnedest," he said.

"Ooh, speaking of trying, we've got to be going. We have another dance class," Jayma said.

"Dance? You guys are going dancing?"

Ugh. Now they were going to think I was a douche. "Guys, guys. Before you start busting my chops, I'd like to let you know that our first date was a dance class. I'd always heard girls love that shit. But it's Jayma who wants to go back for another."

Dig wore a raised eyebrow, and Carter was barely hiding a smirk.

"You guys better watch it or I'll be dragging your asses to the studio for a lesson," Jayma said. Spunky. I liked that.

Dig raised his hands as if he were surrendering to something. "Hey. Each to his or her own. You guys go and enjoy. Twinkletoes."

I HADN'T BEEN VERY psyched about going back to Metronome, since I sucked so badly the first time we went. But Jayma had really wanted to give it another try, so I caved. Shit, who was I fooling? I couldn't say no to her if I'd wanted to.

"So, how'd your meeting with old man Renner go?" I asked her as we drove across town.

"Oh. It went well." She nodded.

"Yeah? That all you're gonna tell me?"

"Well, there's not really much to tell. I mean, Mr. Renner said he might have something for me sometime soon."

"You're kidding! That's great. Aren't you excited?"

She did not seem excited.

"I am. I just can't say much at this point. But I am."

Huh.

"How's work going for *you*?" she asked.

"I don't know. I mean, it's fine. Great, even. My accounts seem happy. But I can't keep up this pace. It's nice I'm getting out tonight, but every other night this week, I'll be working late. I'm getting really burned out."

We drove in silence for a minute.

"You know what? Let's turn around and go back home. Well, to Carter's, I mean," she said.

"What? I thought you wanted to humiliate me with more swing dancing. Are you letting me off the hook?"

She swatted my arm, but I turned the car around before she could change her mind. I didn't care if I never tried swing dancing again in my life. "You're tired. Forget the dancing."

"All right. Hey, how are you feeling about living with a bunch of guys?" I asked her.

"Well, it's kind of weird. We'll see how it goes. I mean, I just don't know about choosing."

I felt for her. I really did. Of course, I hoped she'd choose me. But if she didn't, hell, we'd still be friends and coworkers. I had no doubt about that. A different guy might freak about being in such a predicament, but I was pretty Zen about it. Work was so insane, I didn't have time for any other drama. Whatever happened with Jayma would happen, and I'd always be grateful for the time I had with her. I guess I just wanted her to be happy.

JAYMA

GEEZ, I FELT LIKE CRAP FOR DRAGGING TANNER ACROSS town to something he didn't want to do. What had I been thinking?

Only of myself, apparently.

He did work his freaking ass off. I saw it every day at work. Constant phone calls from clients, meetings both in and out of the office. And his boss was so bitchy.

It would be way more fun for him to just go home and chill—let him get settled into the new place.

Speaking of the new place, how awesome was it that the guys were so cool together? No dick behavior, no puffing their chests out to see who was more of a man. No, just three guys having a sip of some good scotch.

And Wyatt would be joining us shortly.

We got back to the house and headed up to Tanner's

room. On the way, we passed the study, where Carter and Dig were arguing over some sports thing. Something about a player and a coach and who was in the right. It was like a foreign language to me.

"Hey guys, no dancing?" Dig called.

"Nah. We decided to bag it," Tanner answered. "We're headed upstairs."

"Okay, you crazy kids. Have a good night." They returned to their arguing. All I could hear were a lot of "dude" and "douchebag" references. They were in their element.

"I still can't believe this place," Tanner said as we climbed to the second floor. "Carter has done such a good job with it."

It was a really cool house, modern and open, but warm and inviting at the same time. Would the team be able to do something similar to my house next door?

And would they be able to do it fast? Like, really fast? When I thought about it, my future was in their hands. All of their hands.

And their futures were in mine.

"I have an idea," I said to Tanner.

"What's that?"

"Let's take a hot bubble bath together. That'll be super relaxing."

"All right. I never take baths. Let's give it a shot."

We went to crank the hot water over the tub. I ran and grabbed a tiny bottle of bubble bath from my overnight bag and poured the entire thing in the water. The bubbles began to grow like crazy.

"C'mon baby, let's get our clothes off," he said, removing his steamed-up glasses. He reached for the hem of my dress.

Before I knew it, I was standing there in my bra, pink lace panties, and high heels.

"You are fucking gorgeous." His gaze was like velvet, running up and down my body.

"Turn around for me, will you?" he said as he began to remove his own clothes.

I turned my back to him but peeked over my shoulder to catch him eyeing my ass. I backed up so I could rub against him, seeing as he was down to his boxers.

He wrapped his arms around me from behind, running his hands all over my heated skin. I rested my head back on his chest and relaxed into him, savoring his appreciation. I knew it made no sense, but I felt so very close to him. Our connection was powerful—I could have sworn I was falling for him. Legit crazy talk, wasn't it?

I was enveloped in a blanket of warm comfort. Like I'd died and gone to heaven.

"Hey. I've been meaning to ask you. Why do you have musical notes tattooed on your neck?" I asked.

"Oh, I never told you? I used to play in a band. Guitar."

"No way! I had no idea."

He ran his fingers through my hair, slowly getting it wet like the rest of me.

"Yeah. I planned to become a big rock star."

It was funny to think of him that way when I saw him in a suit and his nerdy glasses every day. But when I thought about it more, I could see it. He was, after all, very hunky and handsome. If he lost the suits and grew his hair out...yeah, I could picture him on a stage making ear-splitting music.

"That's kind of hot," I said.

"Well, I think *you're* kind of hot," he replied, running his hands over my breasts and pulling on my nipples until they stood at rock-hard attention. His powerful erection pushed against my back, and I squirmed into it just for fun.

"You think you're clever, don't you?" he asked, nibbling my ear.

"Why? Just because I'm rubbing your hard cock?"

"Mmmm. Yeah."

He reached down between my legs.

"You're so wet. Even in the water, you're slippery as hell down there."

I closed my eyes and relaxed into him. "I guess that's what you do to me."

"You like it, baby?" he growled.

"Mmmm," was all I could manage.

He dragged his fingers up and down my lips, settling on my hard clit. It caused me to suck my breath in small gasps. A tingling sensation shot through me, leaving chilly goose bumps in its wake, even though I was submerged in steamy bathwater.

He abandoned my clit for my aching pussy, where he buried two fingers and started pumping. I braced myself against his rocky chest, my hands on the sides of the tub, and pushed against his hand to deepen the penetration.

"Oh, oh…" I moaned.

"I want to feel you come for me, baby. I want to feel your pussy contract around my fingers. C'mon baby, squeeze me…"

I shook uncontrollably as he pummeled my pussy. He left me gasping, and when I exploded into screams, I didn't care in the least what the rest of the house might have been hearing. My orgasm thundered through me, leaving me shuddering and splashing bathwater all over the place.

Then everything faded to black.

"Baby? You okay?"

"Hmmm? Wha…?"

Tanner was shaking me, gently, by the arms.

"I think you conked out," he said. "C'mon, let's get you out of the water. It's getting cold."

I looked down and found my precious bubbles had

dissolved and the water was no longer warm. He helped me to my feet, and holding my hand, reached for a towel. I awkwardly climbed out of the tub, beginning to shiver from the cold. He grabbed another towel and began rubbing my arms in a vigorous effort to warm me.

"Mmmm. That feels nice," I said.

"I know. Now let's go to bed."

We stumbled into his bed and burrowed beneath a fluffy down comforter. It was like landing in heaven.

"You know what's funny?" I asked.

"What?"

"Well, I was supposed to take care of you tonight. Help you relax."

He wrapped his arms around me and placed a kiss on my forehead.

"Making you feel good makes me feel good," he said.

How did I get this lucky?

I could not believe anything about my crazy situation. I was soaring but also scared to death. Who knew what would happen with my house? Who knew what would happen with the guys? Who knew what would happen with work?

But I did know that I was exhausted and spent, and oh so grateful to be snuggling for the night with my amazing ad man.

173

WYATT

I was all too happy to pitch in on Jayma's house when I got the call from her neighbor, Carter, and when I was invited to move in, I didn't even have to think about it.

I'd be next door to my jobsite.

I'd be under the same roof as my girl.

And I'd get to know the other guys who knocked Jayma's socks off.

Since my dad had been diagnosed with Alzheimer's, I'd had to work my ass off, yes, but I'd also committed myself to living without society's expectations. If that meant the woman I cared for had more than one lover, then so be it. I was not a jealous man. My woman's pleasure, even if it was with another guy, was also my pleasure.

Sometimes this approach was a challenge, I couldn't deny it. I knew it wouldn't be easy to keep a clear head on some nights she was with someone else. But I also knew life was precious, and that "owning" someone was the fastest way to lose them.

I rang the bell to Carter's front door. It wasn't hard to find his place—it was the nice one next to the not-so-nice one that our poor Jayma owned. It was going to feel really good to get in there and begin making some improvements. There was a lot of work, but it was straightforward and didn't have to take long if we were focused and organized. I was all too happy to help my —or should I say *our?*—lovely girl.

The door flew open, and I was greeted by a tall guy with a huge grin.

"You must be Wyatt. Come in, my friend, come in."

"And you must be Carter," I said.

"I am. You are correct. C'mon in and meet the other guys. Hey, can I get you something to drink?" he offered.

"That sounds great. Do you have any beer?"

"I do. Let's go." I followed him through his gorgeous house. Damn, to be a contractor and be able to do anything you want. I mean, being a plumber was certainly useful, but it sure would be handy to know how to do carpentry and everything else, too. But hey, that was why we were teaming up, right?

"Guys, the fourth member of our tribe has arrived," Carter said. "This is Wyatt."

"Hey. Great to meet you guys," I said as they each introduced themselves.

There were handshakes and "cheers" all around. Carter tossed me a cold one.

"So, Wyatt, you're bringing plumbing skills to the table, I've been told," Carter said.

"I am. I look forward to diving in next door."

"So do I. I mean—so do we," Carter said, looking at the other guys.

Tanner, the one with the glasses, spoke up. "Yeah, I'm ready to pitch in, learn a bit of the trade. It'll feel good to do something with my hands other than sit on my ass at a desk and type on a computer keyboard all day."

Dig, the one with the black hair, nodded. "Me too. I mean, I know a little, having worked summers for Carter's dad. But I'm rusty and need a refresher. Just put me to work, guys. I'm all yours."

Carter laughed. "You might be sorry you offered, dude. We may give you all the shit work, ya know."

"Okay. I'm ready," Dig said, laughing.

"So, what's everyone think of our little arrangement?" If I had to be the one to call out the white elephant in the room, I was okay with that.

The guys all looked around at each other.

Who was going to go first?

But we didn't have to wait long.

Dig took a swig of his beer. "Well, Carter and I have been in arrangements like this before."

Tanner turned to him. "No shit. Seriously?"

"We realized we both liked the same woman. When

we talked about it, we didn't see why we both couldn't date her, if that's what she wanted. And she did."

Dig shrugged. "Worked out great."

"Yeah," Carter continued, "some women are into it so they can say they had a threesome. You know, check that off their bucket list. The first woman we dated ended up really falling in love with Dig. I was kind of the third wheel toward the end."

"Yes, she did. I mean, we both loved her back. But when she wanted to be exclusive with me, I just wasn't ready. I was still building my real estate business. Still am, really."

Huh. Intriguing.

"So what do we do when Jayma picks one of us? I mean, isn't that the point of all this?" I asked.

"Sort of," Tanner said. "We all wanted to pitch in and help her with the house. And if one of us ends up with her in the end, we'll wish that guy well. If not, then we'll all be friends. And have some great stories to tell." Everyone laughed.

Dig spoke up. "I was sort of thinking this could be good for business for us, too. Wyatt, Carter, I can refer business to you. I have homebuyers all the time looking for people to work on their houses. And when you see clients getting ready to sell, you keep me in mind."

Carter turned to Tanner. "Sorry dude, but this doesn't exactly do you a lot of good at your ad agency."

"But it does, at least indirectly. If it makes Jayma happy, I'm all over it."

"Cheers to that," everyone said, clinking their beer bottles.

"You guys know my dad used to work on the plumbing next door. I'd been in the house years ago when a Mr. Wagner lived there," I said.

"Wait a minute," Carter said. "Are you Wyatt Deer from Deer Plumbing? Holy shit, I don't know why I didn't put that together. Back in the day, before he passed, my dad and yours referred each other business. How is your dad?"

Ugh. I'd just seen Dad that afternoon. We were losing him fast. And shit, I was in no shape to talk about it.

"Um, well, my dad has Alzheimer's. Pretty bad. I don't think he'll be with us for much longer." I couldn't look up from the floor.

Carter patted me on the back. "Geez, I'm sorry. I had no idea."

"Thank you." Time to change the subject. "So, do we think we can get Jayma's house fixed up before the bank comes for it?"

"Well, she's supposed to hear from them this week about the extension she asked for. If she doesn't get it, we'll be facing a big challenge. I mean, even if we had a crew of a dozen guys, there's only so fast we could move," Carter said.

"If her dickhead boyfriend hadn't stopped paying the mortgage, the timeframe for the reno would not be so compressed. But he basically wore out the goodwill of the bank. And Jayma knew nothing about it until it was too late," Tanner added.

"Anyone ever meet the guy?" I asked, looking at the others.

"I'd see him around, going from his car to the house and back. But he was never friendly. Snooty douchebag," Carter said.

Tanner chimed in. "I'd met him at a couple work functions. He always seemed impressed with himself, if you asked me. Like he thought he was hot shit because he was a lawyer."

"Yeah, real impressive, that one," Dig said. "He couldn't change a goddamn light bulb."

Everyone laughed at that. I couldn't stand guys who were so wussified they wouldn't get their hands dirty. And in my experience, most women felt the same way. If a guy couldn't keep his home up and running, then what fucking good was he?

I guess I was old-fashioned that way.

"Hey guys!"

Jayma had just arrived home from work, and she looked smoking hot, smiling from ear to ear, wearing her career woman clothes with her hair piled up on top of her head. She slayed that sexy librarian thing.

"Damn, baby. Look at you," I said.

A pink tinge ran over her face starting at her neck and finishing at her forehead. I loved that she was humble and so easily embarrassed. I was so over conceited chicks who had nothing else going for them.

If there was one thing I'd learned from watching my parents, you didn't get to keep your looks forever, but you did get to keep your love—if you were fortunate to find it to begin with.

"Hear anything from the bank yet?" Dig asked.

The smile fell from Jayma's face like a heavy rock. "Nah. I'm not sure I'll be hearing from them this week."

Carter shook his head. "What the fuck are they waiting for? I mean, it's your goddamn house. You can't keep people hanging like that."

"Dude, they do it all the time," Dig said. "I see it in my real estate clients. It sucks."

Jayma took a deep breath and forced that smile back on her face. I hated to see her preoccupied with such a downer. I was going to do all I could to turn that hellhole next door into a palace.

"On that note, shall I show you to your room, Wyatt?" she asked.

"Let's do it."

23

JAYMA

When I'd gotten home from work—well, not home, but to Carter's house—and walked in on my guys, I just about fainted. Had I ever seen such a group of perfect men standing together at one time?

And waiting for me?

Hell no. Things like that didn't happen to a girl like me. No, the things that happen to me include shit like getting dumped the very night I thought my boyfriend was going to propose. Getting yelled at by some creepy accountant at work.

Oh, and don't forget a bank that could give a shit about me and my housing situation.

But you know what? I'd come out ahead. I wasn't sure how, but I'd find a way.

And I had four very nice guys on my side. It didn't get much better than that.

In fact, things were looking up at work. I didn't

want to jinx myself, but my meeting with Mr. Renner went well. He was open to my moving off the phones and to working with clients. I didn't know when it would happen, but he seemed to think there'd be an opportunity or two coming up in the near future.

So there was that.

But the guys. My darling guys. They seemed to get along so well. I hoped they became long-term friends, no matter what happened with me.

Speaking of which. How the hell was I going to choose?

No freaking idea.

But I couldn't worry about it at that moment. I had something else to attend to. The last, my Wyatt, had arrived to join the party.

Or freakshow, depending on how you looked at it.

"This is the way upstairs," I said, leading him out of the kitchen. God, he was cute with that dirty blond man bun. I could just picture him backpacking across Europe, with girls dropping at his feet everywhere he went.

Kind of like I wanted to do just then.

I led him up to a room at the end of the hall. It really was pretty amazing of Carter to offer to let all the guys crash at his place. Of course, it made it easier for them to work on my house.

Speaking of which, I couldn't believe how they all wanted to help. Every time I thought about it, I choked up. No one had ever done anything like that for me. No one had ever given me anything so selflessly. No wonder I was falling for them.

Oh, shit. Did I really just say that?

"So what do you think?" I asked, walking into the center of a gorgeous, masculine room that smelled a bit like the crackled leather chair in the corner and the expensive, spicy soap from the bathroom. Clean and manly. Just what the doctor ordered.

Wyatt dropped his bag by the dresser and walked over to me, nodding. His hands ran up to the tangle of curls on top of my head and undid the elastic that held it all together.

"Beautiful. I've never seen such beautiful hair," he murmured, running it through his fingers like he'd discovered gold.

So I reached up and freed his bun, pulling his hair down around his tanned face.

"How is it you get so much color? I'd think that plumbers are inside all day long." I continued to finger his locks. There was no doubt he'd been a beautiful little towhead as a child.

"I take my dad out in his wheelchair twice a day. The sun does him a lot of good. It seems to really cheer him up. He becomes relatively alert, if for only a little while. It almost feels like I'm going to get my dad back." He looked down at the floor.

I took his hand and led him to sit on the edge of the bed.

"It's a hard thing, what you're going through. To see

your dad, who's not really the dad you'd always known, drift away. It must be gut-wrenching."

Gripping my hand, he nodded.

"Hey, I'm sorry. I shouldn't have brought it up," I said.

He looked up at me with tears in his eyes. "No. It's absolutely okay that you brought it up. It sucks, and it's painful, and it's life."

I leaned to kiss his cheek, but he turned just in time for our lips to crash together, slowly, and deeply, building up to something—what, I wasn't sure.

His hands tangled in my hair, and he leaned me back on the bed. My hands wandered down his rock-hard shoulders, along his back, to his muscular ass. He was tall and lanky but so strong. I lost myself in his melting kiss until he pulled away, leaving me panting, to gaze into my eyes.

"I thought about you all day, you know," he growled.

I gasped as his warm hands ran down my hips to clutch the bottom of my skirt. He pulled it up to my waist and cupped and kneaded my ass like he owned it.

He brushed my ear with his lips. "My angel. My beautiful angel."

He made quick work of my clothes, throwing them off the bed, and leaving me in my bra and panties. I shivered as his piercing gaze traced my skin, leaving a trail of goose bumps in its wake.

"Such a pretty girl," he murmured, skimming his

rough hands over my body, only stopping to push my bra aside and tease my nipples.

I arched to give more of myself to him, whimpering when he ground his hard cock into my stomach. He pulled away for a second, righting himself to drop his shirt to the floor, revealing his round pecs and flat tummy. He came back to me, sliding his hands over my belly and to my hips, where he hooked his fingers in the waistband of my panties. The lace whispered over my thighs, joining our other clothing on the floor.

His broad shoulders pushed my legs open as he moved toward my bare pussy. His breath was hot on my core, and at the first flick of his tongue, I started to twist and moan.

"Mmmm…you're nice and wet for me, baby," he whispered, dragging his finger through my lips, capturing the hunger of my dripping pussy.

"God…Wyatt…" I mumbled.

"You feel good, don't you?" he teased, his thumb massaging my clit with small circles.

When he replaced his thumb with his tongue, he dragged it up and down from my clit to my ass, setting me on fire with almost more sensation than I could handle. I twisted and thrashed under him, bucking my hips against his face for more.

I was turning into a greedy little bitch, wasn't I?

His hands reached under me to clutch my ass and he lapped at my aching pussy, driving his tongue as deep inside me as he could. First, my head was spinning, and then it was the entire room. I clawed at the bed for purchase and for the leverage I wanted in order to buck harder against his attentions.

He hopped off the bed, and while I was too twisted up to even lift my head to see what he was doing, I heard a belt come undone, a zipper open, and a tangle of clothing being kicked aside. I managed to peel my eyes open in time to see him climb back between my legs and stroke the thick shaft of his cock. Precum had beaded at the tip. I was dying for a taste, but was too weak to push myself up to my elbows.

"Do you have a condom?" I asked in a croaky voice.

"Yeah, baby," he said, waving around what he already had in his hand. He split open the wrapper and began to unroll it over his length.

His mouth returned to mine, kissing and nibbling my lips, as his cock bounced against my opening. He spread my pussy with one hand and centered his erection, stroking himself while he eased just inside.

I took a deep breath to relax, and he entered me further.

"You okay?" he asked, his gaze burning into my eyes.

God, I felt so connected to him at that moment. It was all so intimate but also sexy as fuck. He stretched my lips wide, driving every inch of his hard dick inside me.

We groaned together, my hands reaching for his ass to pull him closer. He pulled out before plunging back in, holding the sides of my face, brushing my lips, his gaze never leaving mine.

"Oh…oh…god, I'm coming. Yeah, Wyatt, I'm coming…" I called.

His cock continued to piston me, hitting my insides with perfection, his shaft grinding on my clit with every drive. The room spun around me again, and his cock growing even harder. Another stroke and he groaned against my ear, pulling me closer. I clenched around him, moaning and gasping for breath, and we came together.

I was only barely aware of him tucking me into bed under the fluffy down comforter and turning out the lights. He spooned me from behind, sprinkling kisses on my neck and holding me tightly.

All I could think about was how secure I felt with him—and all the guys—as my eyes fluttered closed 'til the next morning.

24

CARTER

Jayma had told me she'd planned to leave work early that day to make good on her promise of serving the guys and me a big family dinner. I had to say, I was psyched at the idea of coming home from work to a house filled with the smells of delicious home cooked food, and even more so, to find a beautiful woman in my kitchen. I'd even bought her a frilly apron to wear. I hoped to see her in it, wearing nothing else, at some point.

But there was plenty of time for that. At least, I hoped there was.

I'd been in traffic over an hour, coming from the home of one of my dad's very first clients. Mrs. Basket must have been pushing ninety, but she was a tough old girl. Her roof had had a leak, and she called, ready to rip me a new asshole about how "today's youth don't know how to do anything right." I explained that her roof was going on thirty years old, and that most roofs lasted only twenty-five if you were lucky. To have one small leak was actually pretty good.

She just scowled at me but gave me half a cake as I was going out the door. The woman cracked me up.

This was my last job before I took a few days to work exclusively on Jayma's house. I'd lined up a couple of my crew, and with Wyatt on the plumbing, and Dig and Tanner on point to do whatever they could, we were in good shape to get the work done well, and done quickly.

The question was, would it be quick enough for the bank? I wasn't so sure about that.

But it was worth a try.

When I pulled into my driveway, I figured I was the last to be arriving, because the house was lit up like a Christmas tree. And just as I'd hoped, the place smelled amazing once I was inside.

It was funny to walk into my home, a place I'd lived alone for a hell of a long time, and find it full of people laughing and having a good time. But I liked it. I really did. It was like coming home to family. It felt warm. And it felt good.

"Hey guys," I said, inching through the three others to get to Jayma. "Hey beautiful." I ran a hand over her ass and planted a big one on her lips.

Her smile was brilliant. "Welcome home, darling."

Tanner handed me a scotch.

"Damn, dude. You're a mind reader," I said, sipping the amber liquid.

He laughed. "I don't know about being a mind reader, but I do remember what you like to drink."

I held my glass up and was joined by the other guys.

"Jayma, grab your glass," Dig said.

"Oh, right." She stopped stirring something on the stove and reached for her glass of red wine.

"Cheers to…renovations," I said.

A round of *cheers to that* followed, and then Jayma shooed us all to the dining room.

"Did everyone have a good day?" Wyatt asked, laughing. "Isn't that what you're supposed to say?"

"No, no. You're supposed to say *honey, I'm home!*" Dig bellowed.

Jayma walked in with a big tray of prime rib that looked like it had been cooked to perfection.

"This all looks so very *Leave it to Beaver*." She laughed.

"Let me help," Wyatt said, jumping from his chair.

Jayma brought the rest of the dinner to the table, and what a feast it was. No one spoke for several minutes while we devoured her excellent cooking.

"To Jayma," Tanner said.

Glasses clinked all around the table, and damn if Jayma's beautiful face didn't turn a bright pink. I liked that about her. Actually, I think we all did.

After some talk about the upcoming baseball

season, I wanted to start the conversation about getting going on Jayma's house.

"So Wyatt, you're available for the plumbing? It looks like the place needs new pipes pretty much across the board. When we open up the walls, I'm thinking you'll be able to dive in, probably day after tomorrow," I said.

"That sounds great, and I have a worker I can bring with me since time's of the essence," he said.

"I've taken a couple days off work," Tanner said. "I can help with the demolition, taking the waste to the dump, etcetera."

"Hey guys, before we go too far down this road, I want to say something." Jayma stood at the end of the table. I didn't like how serious her face looked.

"First, thank you. Thank you for coming together and making a plan to save my house." She looked around the table at each of us, one at a time.

"I got a call today from the bank. They're not giving me any extra time to fix it up and sell it. They just want to foreclose on it. I can't have you put a minute of work into it, knowing that there will be no benefit from it." She looked down at her wine, and when she raised her face to us again, there were tears on her cheeks.

"I just w…wanted you to know…th…that I am more grateful than I can say. You've stepped up to the plate for me in a way I never dreamed anyone would." With that, she fell back into her chair, burying her face in her hands.

"Wait a minute…"

"That's total bullshit…"

"There's got to be something we can do…"

"That fucking bank…"

Everyone was pretty much talking at once, myself included, we were so massively angered by her news.

Dig raised his hands to shush us all. "Hey, hey guys. Hold up. Listen, I don't think we have to take this sitting down. Look, I work in real estate, and I know a little about how these things work. If you have a contract on the house before the bank formally forecloses, that halts the proceedings."

Jayma pulled her hands away from her face. "Really? But do you think we could get someone? We can't show the house in the condition it's in right now."

"I completely agree," Dig said, looking around at the guys. "But from what Carter says, we have a good shot at doing the reno pretty fast. You already have the permits for the work, and I know someone at the city inspector's office who'll get us on the calendar for inspection. I still think there's a chance we can pull it off."

The guys all nodded. Jayma was unconvinced.

"You all have already been so good to me. I can't let you do something that will most likely end up having been a waste of your time."

Tanner shrugged. "I don't see how it's a waste of time. It sounds like a great challenge and speaking for myself, I look forward to learning from these guys. I'm tired of talking about tampons all day."

All heads whipped in Tanner's direction.

"Dude, what the hell are you talking about?" Wyatt asked.

Tanner rolled his eyes. "I'll explain another time. I just want it to be known that I'm still in if you guys are."

I knew *I* was. I believed we had a chance. I looked at Wyatt and Dig. It was clear they weren't backing down that easily, either.

"C'mon Jayma. Let's give it our best shot. You've got a helluva crew here," I said, looking around at the guys.

"I…I don't know. I just don't know," she said in a quiet voice.

Dig was the first on his feet. He walked to the end of the table where Jayma sat and pulled her into his arms.

"Baby, it's not over 'til it's over. And it ain't over yet."

As soon as dessert was finished and we'd cleared the table, I headed to bed. I didn't know who Jayma spent the night with, if anyone, and it didn't matter. All I wanted to do was climb into bed for a good night's rest.

I planned to get up early to get to work on her house. I'd make sure we proved to her that we'd do our best, for as long as she gave us the opportunity to.

25

JAYMA

How did I get so lucky? Or was it unlucky? Depended how you looked at it, I suppose.

The guys were going to bust their asses. For me. In spite of the fact that it could end up being all for naught. How could I ever repay them? Certainly not by choosing one to be with and cutting the others loose.

Yeah, some kind of nice that would be. I'd go off with one of the guys, and the others would be shit out of luck.

How would that be good for any of us?

But I'd worry about that later. First, I had to get through a shitty day at work. Bob, the douche from finance, had already been out in reception, scolding me about not having made his copies fast enough. Apparently he'd forgotten about Tanner's threat.

"You know, Jayma, I have my meeting starting pretty soon. I really need my stuff," he said.

Did I say he was a dick? And that he also needed to trim his nose hairs?

Thank goodness he didn't meet with clients.

"Bob, I'll have them done in time. The phone's been ringing off the hook, and you know that has to be my top priority."

His face turned into a scary shade of red. Maybe he'd explode. It would be a mess, but then at least he'd be off my ass.

"I'm not leaving until you do them, Jayma. Please get on it."

"Jayma speaking," I answered the phone. I gave him the *just a minute* finger signal but he chose to ignore it.

Fucking asshole.

"Jayma, goddamn it—" But he didn't get to finish.

The door to the reception area flew open.

It was Tanner. He didn't look happy.

You might think it was weird, having a "thing" with someone from work, but instead of it being awkward, as I had thought it would be, it was strangely comforting.

"Bob, I can hear your big goddamn mouth all the way down the hall in my office. Is there some reason you can't make your own copies?" He got close to Bob's face. *Really* close. Probably *too* close.

"You know, Webb, you need to mind your own business." Wow, I didn't know Bob had it in him. I didn't like the guy, but I had to hand it to him, he was standing up for himself. Even if he was in the wrong.

As the volume of their voices increased, I cupped my hand over my headset's mic so no one on the phone would hear the shit show unfolding in front of me.

Tanner pulled his shoulders back and puffed out his chest the way guys do when they're trying to look tough. And boy, did he pull it off. Tough guy with slightly nerdy glasses. I didn't know whether to be terrified or to take out my cell phone and snap a picture.

"It *is* my business—the whole office's business—when we hear you raising your voice," Tanner said with gritted teeth.

Bob's face was purple at this point, and sweat was beading on his temples. He snatched his papers off my desk, pointing a finger into Tanner's chest.

"I wouldn't be having a meeting about all this," he violently shook his fistful of paper, "if the accounts you worked on were making the company some money."

Oops.

"What did you say?" Tanner asked.

Oh shit. Shit. Shit. Shit.

I was frozen in place. I knew I should be calling someone for help before all hell broke loose, but I was in panic mode, and therefore mostly useless.

Just then, Mr. Renner appeared in the reception area's doorway.

"What the hell's going on out here?" He snapped us all out of our adrenaline-charged trance. Both Bob and Tanner backed away from each other.

Tanner spoke first. "I think there may have been a small misunderstanding about responsibilities, but it's all straightened out now. Right, Bob?" he asked, looking right at him.

"Um, yes. Yes, it's all good." Bob rushed past Mr. Renner in the doorway, disappearing down the hall.

Mr. Renner approached Tanner and me. "Is everything okay here?"

We bobbed our heads in unison, uttering all forms of *yessir's, everything's great.* Tanner headed back to his office, after a sly wink at me.

"Jayma, I'd like to talk to you in my office. Can you get one of the girls to cover for you?" Without waiting for my answer, he turned and left.

Ohmygod. Shit. Was I in trouble?

I got someone to answer the phones and tore down the hallway to Mr. Renner's office with a pad and pen in hand.

"Mr. Renner?"

"Jayma, yes, come in and please close the door." He gestured toward the seat opposite his desk.

Good lord. Was this my last day at work? Because if it was, I'd have much bigger problems than just my house being foreclosed on.

Who knew my life could get more fucked up than it already was?

"Jayma, the other day you approached me with your interest in taking on more responsibility. Growing your career here at the agency." He looked down at his hands, which were folded on his desk.

I wished he would have just dispensed with the niceties. If I was being shit-canned, I wanted to know right away so I could pack up my stuff and get the hell out.

But I wasn't going down easy.

"Yes, Mr. Renner. I really feel I have a lot to contribute and some very creative ideas about pulling in new business and serving the clients we currently have." God, if that didn't sound like corporate suck-up talk, I didn't know what would. But it was true. I did have some damn good ideas.

I thought of the guys at home—well, at Carter's home—who seemed to really believe in me and who wanted to make me succeed against the odds of foreclosure. A wave of conviction welled up in me, and I found myself sitting ramrod straight in my chair. If Mr. Renner didn't want my contribution, then I'd take my ideas elsewhere.

Give me your worst, Mr. Renner.

He took a deep breath and met my gaze. "I have something to talk to you about, Jayma."

IT WAS ALL I could do to keep my eyes on the road on my way home. I'd gotten someone to cover the phones and left early to clear my head. My hands had been shaking so hard when I got in my car that it took me five minutes to get my seat belt buckled. I turned on some calming music and took deep breaths. They say you should never drive when you're worked up, but what if you have somewhere to go?

I pulled up at Carter's and used my key to quietly enter. I wasn't up for talking with any of the guys, if they were even home. I peered out of his kitchen window toward my house. It sounded like there was plenty going on with them all over there, anyway.

I ran up the stairs two at a time to my bedroom and closed the door behind me. Sitting on the edge of the bed, I rooted through my purse for my phone, fighting back tears. My hands shook so badly, I had trouble pulling up Shelle's number.

It was such a relief that she answered right away.

"Hey girl!" she yelled. I could hear waves and seagulls in the background. She must have brought the dogs to the beach. I tried not to picture them crapping all over the sand.

"Shelle, you won't believe what happened at work," I said, trying to steady my voice.

"Yeah? What's up?"

"Well, Mr. Renner, the founder of the agency, offered me a job."

Not one where I had to answer phones and make copies for assholes like Bob. No, he'd offered me a big, fat, motherfucking *real* job.

THE RENOVATION

26

TANNER

Something was up. Jayma had bolted out of work and then texted us all to gather for a "family dinner." I guess we were sort of like a family. Dig had to reschedule a couple meetings, so he was expected to be somewhat late, but everyone else would be there, no problem.

Personally, I could have stayed at work longer. I had a ton of stuff to do on the damn tampon account. We were just wrapping up our research on how we stacked up against the competition, and I was quickly becoming the male expert on "flow." Boy, could I talk about menstruation now.

Great topic of conversation for the next cocktail party I attended.

Yeah…no.

Christ, that accounting asshole Bob had pissed me off. I mean, even if I hadn't been romantically involved with Jayma, I still would have stuck up for her. I fucking hated bullies. I was always ready to take them on.

That's why I had a little scar above my right eyebrow. But that was a long story involving neighborhood kids and a little weakling with glasses. Who finally learned to stand up for himself.

And yeah, that kid was me.

I pulled up at Carter's and was blown away by all the activity next door. Someone had delivered a giant dumpster very early in the morning, and by god, it was already nearly full. Those guys weren't messing around. I'd be pitching in over the weekend, and I had a feeling Carter and Wyatt were going to work my ass *hard*.

I didn't want to get in the way of the assembly line of workers he had pulling waste and other construction debris out of the house in one wheel barrow-full after another, but I was dying to see what was going on. I jumped out of the way of the latest worker to come flying out the door and poked my head inside.

"Carter!" I called.

"Yo. Up here," he answered.

The once-rickety handrail on the staircase was now completely gone, so I walked up hugging the wall, which looked like someone had pounded the shit out of it with a sledge hammer. Which they apparently had, as evidenced by the one leaning against the wall at the top of the stairs.

"Wow," I said, once I'd found Carter. "You weren't kidding when you said you could move fast. Good grief. There's not much left of the place."

He wiped the sweat from his forehead and looked around. "Yeah, we've pretty much gutted everything except Jayma's bedroom." He pointed toward a closed door sealed off with a large sheet of plastic. She'd be very happy the construction dust was being kept out of the one good room in the house.

"So," I said, "another family dinner tonight? Is something up? Do you know?"

He shrugged. "No idea. I got Jayma's text and said I'd be there. You're coming, right?"

"Oh yeah, for sure. I'm just going to grab a run and shower in time for dinner."

"All right, man. I'll see ya later. Hey, when can I put your lame ass to work?" he asked with a laugh.

"Ha, funny guy. I'll be getting down to work here on the weekend. And I'll *try* not to show you up. No promises, though." I gave him the finger as I left.

How was it I was already so comfortable with someone I'd only just met? It was the strangest thing when I thought about it, but he was such a cool guy, it was easy to like him. Actually, they were all good guys. We all liked the same woman, and there were no jealousy issues. I guess we all wanted what was best for Jayma and weren't going to let our own insecurities get in the way.

When I got back from my run, I heard someone

banging around in the kitchen. Sure enough, there was my Jayma, cooking up a storm like she had a few nights before. I sneaked up behind her, grabbing her around the waist, and planting a kiss on her cheek.

"Ack, you scared me, silly boy," she said, turning in my arms to plant a big one on my lips.

I took a step back to admire her. "Hey, you ran out of work early. Everything okay?"

She nodded. "Um, yeah. Everything's good. I just needed a little time to myself. Thank you for chasing Bob off."

"That guy is such a dick. I don't know why Renner keeps him around."

"Well, I don't think he means any harm. He's trying to get his shit done like everyone else. He just doesn't know how to ask in a way that makes anyone want to help him out."

"So what's the family meeting about? Something up?" I asked.

Jayma turned back to stirring something on the stove. "No. Not really. Just wanted to talk with everyone."

Something was definitely up. But if she wasn't ready to talk, I was good with that.

"Okay, baby. I'm running upstairs for my shower."

"Dinner's in one hour. Be on time," she said with a smile.

"Yes, ma'am. I'd never be late for one of your dinners."

Not forty-five minutes later, Carter, Wyatt, and I were sitting in the living room, all showered and shaved, downing some beers, and waiting on Dig.

"One of the coolest things about reno'ing a house is getting to see how they did construction back in the day," Carter said. "All that lath and plaster they used to build walls. Incredible. It took so much work. Unlike the drywall we slap up today."

"How'd the house end up in such bad condition, anyway?" I asked.

"Not sure. I guess Wagner, the guy who lived there before Jayma bought it, had just gotten old and eccentric. Plaster falling off the ceiling must not have bothered him," Carter said, shaking his head.

"Well, you've done an incredible job with *this* place, Carter," Wyatt said, looking around. "I can only imagine how Jayma's house will be when you're done with it."

"Ha. What do you mean when I'm done with it? You'll both be busting your asses on the place soon. I'm not gonna do it all on my own."

"Now that you've got the walls down, I'll dive into the plumbing tomorrow," Wyatt said.

Dig came flying in the house. "Guys. Am I late?" he asked breathlessly.

"No man. Go get a beer."

"So Carter, how long you letting us all live at your house?" I asked.

"Well, the idea was to let Jayma see which of us she wants to be with in the long-term."

Dig settled into the sofa. "But Carter and I are a package deal."

"Do I hear you guys talking about me?" Jayma called from the living room entrance.

She was wearing some sky-high heels and a pretty little halter dress that revealed almost all of her back. The red hair tumbling down against her fair skin was stunning. I held out my hand.

"Dinner will be ready in just a few minutes. Hi Tanner," she said, snuggling into my lap.

I did a quick inventory of the other guys' faces to see how they felt about me helping myself to our girl, but they all looked completely cool with it.

She looked at the other guys and leaned down to give me a soft and juicy kiss that I didn't think I'd ever forget. Then, she looked back around. Our baby clearly liked being watched.

"Okay, guys. Show's over," she said, popping up from my lap.

Groans echoed around the room.

"C'mon. Dinner time."

Once again, Jayma served a dinner that blew me away.

She was a keeper, for sure. Question was, who'd end up with her?

"I wanted to say something to the four of you," she said, standing up.

The expression on her face was pretty serious. Could it have to do with whatever went down at work earlier? Christ, I hope there wasn't some sort of problem.

"I think you all know—Tanner does for sure, since we work together—that I've been receptionist at the ad agency for a long time now. Well, I wanted to share with you that the founder, Mr. Renner, called me into his office today."

Oh shit. Was she in trouble over the Bob thing? Had I made it worse?

"And," she looked around the table, "he told me he liked my work ethic, and that he wanted me to be part of the account team. He offered me a great new job!"

The table erupted in cheers, which she quieted by waving her hands.

"There is a, um, complication, though," she said.

We all looked at each other, then back at her.

"What sort of complication?" Wyatt asked.

A strange sadness washed over her face.

"The position isn't here in San Francisco."

"So where is it, baby? Down in Silicon Valley? That's not that far," I said.

She looked around the table at each of us.

"No, the job is in Chicago."

27

JAYMA

"What?"

"You're fucking kidding."

"They couldn't find you a job here in California?"

The questions came at me like a driving rain. I had known they would, though.

I'd thought Mr. Renner was throwing me out on my ass. But he offered me a job in the Chicago office working on a new account. He said he liked the idea of someone from the home office being there.

I'd just about fallen off my chair when he said that. Then I nearly cried. But I held it together until our meeting was done. It was then that I had to run to the bathroom, where I got sick.

But what an incredible break. Life had been so shitty, with Lance taking off, and then the house going into foreclosure.

An incredible break. Right. My dream job.

In another fucking city.

The universe was having one big, huge laugh at my expense.

"Are you really going?"

"What timeframe are you looking at?"

"Do you *have* to go?"

More questions were lobbed at me. Questions I didn't have answers to. But I owed these guys responses. I owed them way more than that, actually.

"I leave at the end of this month."

Saying those words felt like someone reaching down my throat and tearing out my heart. I could hardly believe I was even able to spit them out.

"Why? Why are you going?" Dig asked. The look on his face made me want to run away.

"The main reason is," I took a slow look around the room, "that I've fallen for all of you. And I can't eliminate anyone. So, I'm leaving town. I'll be alone, and my house will probably have been foreclosed on, but at least I won't bear the burden of hurting any of you by making a choice."

"You think it won't hurt us that you're leaving?" Tanner asked, pulling off his glasses to rub his eyes.

"I know it probably will. But not as much as if I made a choice and rejected anyone. I can't do it. I won't do it."

A lump slowly built in my throat. Dammit, the last thing I wanted was to be a crybaby in front of the guys.

"Jayma, you don't have to leave town. Stay here. We'll figure it out," Carter said.

Everyone around the table nodded. They'd all put their forks down a while ago and dinner was now cold.

"Please, guys. I've made my mind up. Let's finish eating."

But dinner was over.

"HEY! OVER HERE!" Shelle called. She had only three dogs with her. Light day, it looked like.

I ran to catch up to her in the dog park, watching where I stepped in the hope of avoiding dog poo. I had to go directly to work from here and couldn't drag dog shit into the office.

"Good morning. Fancy you being out here so early." She didn't look happy with me.

Hell, I wasn't so sure I was happy with me, either.

"So. You're out of here? Leaving on a jet plane, as they say?" she asked, avoiding my gaze.

"Don't know what else to do."

"The old balance of job versus love. Either way you go, you'll have some sort of regret," she said, putting a hand on my arm. It was clear she'd been ready to give me all levels of shit, but when she saw how torn up I was, she backed off.

I couldn't hold it in any longer and exploded into sobs. "I…I…it's…so…messed…up."

Shelle led me to a bench and sat me down, her arm around my shoulders.

"C'mon," she said. "Let it out."

I buried my face in her shoulder, covering her fleece with my snot and tears. But she wouldn't care. She was on my side, no matter what I did.

I pulled myself up and blew my nose on the tissue she'd handed me.

"You could come with me, you know," I told her.

Yeah, right. Fat chance. No one in San Francisco would move to Chicago unless they absolutely had to.

She looked down. "I don't know, Jayma. I don't think I could. I mean, Chicago's so cold…"

"I know," I said, catching my breath and nodding. ""I feel bad. The guys are working so hard on the house. They've been so good to me."

"And you're leaving town…*why?*"

"Well, one, for the job, but mainly because I can't choose among the guys. I like them all, Shelle. Wyatt, the quieter one with that crazy man bun, takes such good care of his dad. I love that about him. Then there's Tanner from work, with his Mad Men glasses. He's helped me so much with my career by mentoring me. Dig, Mr. Italian Stallion, wants to sell my house for me before the bank takes it, and his best friend Carter, my blue eyed guy, is leading the charge to renovate the place."

It was true. I could never choose, because there was something about each of them that was just incredible. I wanted them all. Like that was a possibility. Maybe in another universe.

"Who's better in bed?" Leave it to Shelle to ask that.

But to be honest, I'd asked myself that, too.

And I couldn't answer it.

"They're all great. Each one in his own way. I can honestly say that I've never had sex before like I have had with those guys. Each one is different. And each one's amazing."

"When are you leaving?" she asked.

"I'm supposed to be there within the month." I turned to her. "I don't feel like I should stay at the house with the guys any more. Can I come stay with you?"

"Of course you can, sweetie. You can stay as long as you like. I'll send the dogs to my parents' house. You can bring your cat." She held my hand.

"Thanks, Shelle. I knew I could count on you."

"Of course, sweetie. Always." She pulled me into an embrace. I didn't know what I was going to do without her.

As MUDDLED as my head was, it actually felt good to get

to work. I was dying for something to occupy my brain.

But when I got there, I realized that was not to be.

My desk was covered in four giant vases of flowers.

Shit.

And, the tears were back.

I plopped down at my desk in reception, wishing I didn't have to sit in such a public place when I felt so shitty.

Mr. Renner passed through on the way to his office. "Well, look at all the flowers you've got. You have some very nice friends, helping you celebrate your new job this way."

He was right. I did.

Tanner wandered in next.

"Hey," he said quietly.

"Hey," I said back. "Does everybody hate me?"

He laughed. "If everybody hated you, do you think they'd send you flowers?"

Ugh. That goddamn lump was back in my throat.

He looked around to make sure we were alone. "Baby, don't beat yourself up. Everyone respects your decision. We may not like it. It may not be what we would do. But you have to do what feels right."

Shit. There went one tear, rolling right down my cheek. One from my other eye quickly followed.

"This is hard on you," Tanner said.

Oh, why did he have to be so nice?

"But we're here for you. *I'm* here for you. I always will be, no matter what."

I swallowed hard and nodded. It was about all I could do.

When he was gone, I contemplated opening the flowers' cards right then or saving them until later. I pulled them all out of the arrangements and held the little white envelopes, each so small, but each brimming with the promise of love.

Love that I was walking away from.

I tore open the envelopes, one at a time, letting the ripped paper flutter to the floor.

Each of these petals is a kiss I'm sending you—Carter
You've stolen my heart—Dig
You have brought so much to my life—Wyatt
You take my breath away—Tanner
Well, shit.

2 8

WYATT

I think all us guys took the news from Jayma okay. We weren't happy about it, and speaking for myself, I didn't get a wink of sleep that night. Not sure anybody in the house did.

She did her best to talk us out of the house renovation, but we couldn't be swayed. She figured she'd just let the bank take it, and that would be the end of it, but we had different plans. With Carter heading up the reno, and Dig the sale, I was feeling pretty good about her getting her money back and then some. It was a good challenge, and it was always great to tell a bank to take a hike.

Plus, I really liked all the guys. We were a good group. With Jayma in the picture or not, I figured we'd still hang out. So all was not lost.

We'd had a couple days to think over what her move meant. She'd taken her stuff and gone over to her friend's house, so that left things pretty subdued. But it had given us time to come up with a plan while we continued the renovation.

We'd asked her to come back over to Carter's to talk. I wasn't surprised she agreed. I figured she missed us as much as we missed her.

I was just finishing up for the day at her house. The plumbing wasn't in horrible shape, per se, it was just old and a lot of the pipes needed replacing. When the walls were all open and you could easily get to anything you want, the job would go pretty fast.

Being in her house and wondering if I'd ever see her again was playing a trip on my head. When no one was around, I slipped behind the huge sheet of plastic that closed off her bedroom and sneaked into her room. I closed the door behind me and sat down on her bed.

The room looked and smelled just like her. Like the Jayma I knew and loved.

Shit. Did I just say love?

Fuck, was I in trouble.

There was a fresh, clean scent to the room, which was decorated in what my mom would call "neutral tones." There was a lot of gray and white, and while that sounds boring as hell, I have to tell you, it was real soothing. I ran my hand over the down comforter on her bed, imagining she was in here with me.

God, I was turning into a pussy.

When I was coming out of the room, I ran smack into Carter. I must have looked embarrassed as hell.

"Dude," he said, "I did the same thing yesterday. I went in her room just to…feel close to her for a moment."

So I wasn't the only one.

"Yeah…" I didn't know what else to say.

Carter put his hand on my shoulder. "What do you say we head out? We gotta get showered up before Jayma comes over."

"Yeah. It's been a long day. We got a shitload done," I said, looking around the place. I loved that everyone saw the potential in the house. With a bit of polishing, it would be quite the gem.

The challenge now was our race against the clock.

WE GUYS WERE in the living room, trying to relax, but the conversation was light. The doorbell rang, and Dig jumped up to answer it.

"You don't have to ring the bell, sweetie," he said, kissing her on the cheek.

I wanted to kiss her, too, but it was time to be patient. If it was meant to be, that would come later. That, and more.

After hellos were said and Jayma had a glass of wine in her hand, Carter took the lead. It was his house and his idea to have her back over.

He stood for the occasion.

"Jayma, we have a proposition for you, all four of us do." He looked around the room, and we nodded at him to continue.

She sat with her legs crossed, her back ramrod straight. There was no hiding that she was just as nervous as we were.

Carter continued, "As you have probably noticed, none of us is thrilled about the idea of your moving to Chicago. We're happy about your promotion—the move, not so much." He took a sip of his scotch.

"We understand why you want to leave us, and that you feel you can't move forward without hurting someone. That's very decent of you. Wouldn't you agree, guys?" He looked around. Our nodding heads answered his question.

Jayma's face was deathly white, and her wine glass was shaking in her hand.

"So what we want to say to you, darling, is that you don't *have* to choose."

As she let the news sink in, confusion crossed her face in a furrowed brow. "Huh? What do you mean? I don't get it."

"We love you, Jayma."

There was a chorus of *yes, we do,* as her eyes widened.

"And we all want to be with you. We don't want you to choose. We want to share you. All four of us."

"I don't get it," she said. Her eyes were filling with tears. Shit, mine were, too.

"If you'll have us, we'd like you to move back in. Come live with us."

"Like, be with all of you?" she asked, looking at each of us.

"Speaking for myself, I think it would be hot as shit," Dig said with his usual big smile.

"Yeah? What about you, Wyatt, and you, Tanner?"

"We're totally down with it. It would be great to know that there's always someone looking after you when we're not around," I said.

Carter nodded. "Thanks to your bringing us together—or should we thank your friend Shelle?—Wyatt and I are going to partner in our work. Most jobs we do require the skills we both bring to the table. Dig, as he builds his clientele, is going to send more and more clients our way. Things could really explode."

"Where does that leave Tanner?" she asked.

He reached from his seat to take her hand. "Jayma, what would you say to you and me opening our own small boutique firm?"

"What? Can we do that?" she asked.

"Actually, I've discussed it with Mr. Renner. He has more business than he can handle and would love to send some of the smaller clients my way. If you joined me, we'd be doing our own thing but partnering with him at the same time."

"Are you kidding?"

"Absolutely not. It's up to you, but you now have options. Mr. Renner will support you, I know he will."

With a rush of emotion, her bottom lip quivered, and tears ran down her cheeks. We all rushed to her, surrounding her like we were her harem.

She mumbled something I didn't catch. It didn't look like any of the other guys did, either.

"What was that, sweetie? We couldn't hear you," I said.

"I said okay. Okay, I'll stay with you guys." Her voice was wobbly through the tears.

"I love all of you, too. I really do." She blew her nose and laughed.

"I'm in. I'm all in," she said.

29

JAYMA

WHOA.

They all wanted me. And I wanted all of them. So I decided to jump in with my heart open wide.

What's the worst that could happen?

I'd end up out on my ass with a house in foreclosure...

Oh, wait, that had already happened to me.

I wanted to tell myself it was a crazy, silly idea, and that it would never work. That it was wrong, or dirty, or something terrible like that.

But the thing was...it didn't *feel* wrong. It felt natural. It felt smart. It felt safe.

The minute I said *yes*, I was surrounded by all the guys. The air around me was warm, really warm, and my pulse was slamming every inch of my body.

All four of the guys—*my* guys—remained completely silent while their eyes blazed into me.

"Hey, do you guys think—"

But I never got to finish. Dig pulled me into him, his lips searing mine with a fierceness that momentarily scared me. I moaned into his mouth as I felt six more hands on my body. A pair of lips fell on my neck; someone was unzipping my dress and someone else was removing my shoes.

A girl could get used to this.

And I planned to.

Holy shit. This was really happening.

But I was ready and I was turned on. I'd never wanted anything so much in my life.

My clothes were peeled off, and I was laid out on the soft rug on the floor. All around me, the guys were dropping their clothes, too, and in an instant, I was surrounded by gorgeous men with ripped abs, powerful arms, and four very hard—and very large —cocks.

You know that kid in a candy store feeling?

Yeah, I know you do.

"Are you in, baby? It's not too much?" Tanner asked.

I looked around at all my loves and gasped, "I'm yours. All of yours." I pulled Tanner into a kiss.

I heard soft conversation after that, and I might have even said a few things myself, although I don't remember much besides the expectation of where eight talented hands were going to take me. I shivered in anticipation, goose bumps exploding over my body. I moaned as Wyatt took his turn kissing me. I lost track of who was doing what when my eyes fluttered closed. My back arched to push my nipples into somebody's mouth, and two of the others positioned my legs wide apart. Kisses began to run up both my calves and then inner thighs. I was lost in the heat of it all.

Somebody's tongue found its way to my pussy and dragged slowly—agonizingly slowly—through my slit, pushing aside my lips to give more access. Pleasure burst through me in a spike just as my nipples were squeezed and twisted to the point of pain. I felt a piece of fabric on my head and Carter—I could tell his voice anywhere—asked if I was okay with a blindfold.

Hell, yeah.

He gently pulled what felt like a sleep mask over my eyes, and the sensations running through me multiplied. There were mouths and hands of four amazing men making me feel like a queen.

A finger entered me, followed by another, pumping slowly. A mouth landed on my clit and drew it between lips that were pillowy and forceful at the same time. I writhed on the floor, all sensation magnified because I couldn't see.

"How are you, baby?" Dig's voice whispered in my ear.

"Mmmm…good," was about all I could manage.

"Okay, darling. Because we're gonna make you feel better than you ever have in your life."

Someone's mouth, wet from my pussy, ran over my

own. I loved the taste and smell and opened my greedy mouth for more.

Everything—all of it—was unlike anything I'd ever experienced. Every single inch of my being was taken care of by my boys, making me feel like I might shatter under the pleasure of it all. Someone's dick was placed in my hand, and I began to stroke it. Another found its way to my mouth, and the fingers in my pussy were replaced by a cock that entered me very slowly, a little bit at a time, allowing me to adjust. On the other side, I felt the rhythm of someone stroking himself into my breasts.

When one of them was fully seated inside me, I was rocked by the motion of fucking. At the other end, I held someone's balls, directing a cock in and out of my hungry mouth until my cheeks hollowed. The pressure inside me built like an ember about to spark into a roaring fire.

"Come for us, beautiful," Wyatt murmured in my ear. "We want to see you come."

I was surrounded by sensation, and moaning—so much moaning. A thick, hot stream of semen landed on my breasts, accompanied by a loud growl. The load was abundant and ran off me on to the rug below.

The pounding in my pussy was fevered, and the cock in my mouth pistoned until my lovers came in me at the same time.

Holy fuck.

I pounded my one empty fist on the floor as an

orgasm shattered over me. Even though I had the mask over my eyes, there were flashes of light while my entire body spasmed. I'd never come like that, not even close. But then, I'd never been with four men at once.

I gasped for air as the guys around me did the same, me still full of cock on both ends, and now in my hands, as well.

And all I could think about was how I wanted to do it again.

I pulled the mask off my eyes and what a sight to behold. Four of the most fucking gorgeous men walking the face of this earth were all hovering over me, admiring me, loving me, and taking care of me.

And this was just the beginning.

30

DIG

True to his word, Carter pulled off Jayma's house reno with time to spare. That guy was a fucking rockstar, no doubt about it. He'd even fronted the money for everything.

I walked through the place one last time before the open house I'd scheduled, which promised to bring in a shitload of hungry buyers. I hoped they had a lot of cash—or at least good credit—'cause this baby was going to go for a pretty penny.

The walls were new. The floors were new. The lighting, electrical, and plumbing were new. We'd installed updated wainscoting, picture rail, molding, cabinets, appliances—you name it—the place was a stunner. They'd even fixed the foundation and dry rot. I knew there'd be a lot of folks dying to get into a home as clean as this one.

Jayma, of course, was beside herself. I could tell,

though, that she was a little sad that she'd never get to live in the house in its pristine state. That dream had not come true. But hopefully her new life with us outweighed any disappointment. I was pretty sure it did.

I put the *open house* signs out front, and Jayma brought over home baked cookies and lemonade for our visitors. We were leaving nothing to chance. We had two days to get a contract on the house in order to fend off the vultures that called themselves a bank.

The work that had been done on the house would also serve as a sort of calling card for Carter and Wyatt's new home building partnership. The work they did together was the best you could find in the entire Bay Area. I was already sending my clients to them, and they were sending referrals to me. Good news all around.

As Tanner had planned, he and Jayma were leaving the ad agency, with the blessing of its owner, to hang out their own shingle for a new, boutique-style firm. Mr. Renner had thrown a few small clients their way, but we were all most excited about the work they were going to do for Carter and Wyatt's new business. It really was kind of wild how things had just fallen into place. Life was funny that way. You'd be beating your head against the wall over and over, trying to achieve something, and then one day, things just *worked*. They fell into place as if they'd always been there. Maybe they had, and we'd been just too close—or too dumb—to see it.

We were all getting to know Jayma's crazy friend Shelle, too. Every now and then, she'd come over to Carter's house—now *our* house—with a carload of dogs. She'd set them loose in the backyard and they'd go wild sniffing everything before settling down. Of course, we locked the cat in the house, first. Tanner and Jayma were going to help Shelle promote her business, too, although she was doing so well, I don't see how she could handle more customers. Or dogs.

After two days of open houses, we had twenty offers. Jayma chose the one that would settle the fastest and paid off the note on the house with mere hours to spare.

How often does that happen?

She was able to repay Carter the money he'd fronted for the reno, too, and then pocket what was left. So against all odds, she managed to make some money on that damn house.

Don't you know the douchebag ex-boyfriend came sniffing around when he found she'd done well with the sale of the house. But he didn't have a goddamn leg to stand on, even though he whined like a baby about "all the money he put into the place."

My ass. I kicked him the hell out and told him to never return. He slunk off like a little kid who'd been scolded.

We celebrated with some fancy champagne for

Jayma and some very high-end scotch for us guys. There were tears in her eyes when she thanked us. And then she told us she loved us.

She loved us. Each of us.

And we loved her right back.

The five of us had all sorts of ways to have fun, but that celebratory night we were engaging in our favorite.

Badminton.

Yes, we loved badminton. Especially naked badminton.

We'd just finished an exceptionally good meal courtesy of Jayma's incredible cooking. She went fishing in the front closet, pulling out five racquets and a bag of birdies.

"Who's game?" she squealed, jumping up and down.

God, I love when she did that.

Carter and Wyatt were the first ones on their feet. Their clothes were off in a matter of seconds, laying in piles around their feet. Tanner was quick to follow, as was Jayma.

"C'mon!" she screamed, running for the nicely private backyard where Carter had put up a net. The guys went running after her.

I shook my head and laughed, also dropping trou for the game. I ran to catch up to the rest of the guys and the woman we'd made our queen.

And who'd made us her kings.

Did you like *The Renovation*?
Check out the next book *in the* steamy
Contemporary Reverse Harem Collection
THE PROMOTION

I hope you loved reading this book as much as I
loved writing it.
Find all Mika Lane books here:

https://mikalaneshop.com/

Dear Reader:

I'm USA TODAY bestselling romance author Mika Lane, and am OBSESSED with bringing you sassy, steamy stories with imperfect heroines and the bad-a*s dudes they bring to their knees. I'll always bring you my signature humor and heat, topped off with a modern-day happily ever after.

My first book ever was *The Day I Ate the Milkyway*, a true fourth-grade masterpiece illustrated with crayons and bound with construction paper and glue. Nowadays, steamy romance gives purpose to my days and nights as I create worlds and characters that tickle the imagination. I live in magical Northern California with my own handsome alpha dude, sometimes known as Mr. Mika Lane, and two devilish cats named Chuck and Murray.

A dual citizen of the United States and Ireland, I have on more than one occasion spent my last dollar on a plane ticket somewhere, and am always planning my next escape. I often try new recipes on unsuspecting friends, search out hiding places to read undisturbed, and sadly kill every houseplant I bring home.

I LOVE to hear from readers when I'm not dreaming up naughty tales to share. Visit my online shop https://mikalaneshop.com/ and say hello https://mikalaneshop.com/pages/meet-mika.

xoxo, Mika